LYING BASTARD

a novel

CLINT MARGRAVE

ISBN: 978-1-7333526-1-1
Run Amok Books, 2020
First Edition

RunAmok

Printed in the USA

Lying Bastard

by

Clint Margrave

LYING BASTARD

Instructor: Berlin Saunders
Spring 2008
Time: 10:25-11:40 a.m.
Days: MW

Class: HUM 302
Office: N/A
Office Hours: N/A

Part 1: Introduction to the Class

Week 1
Chapter 1: O Captain! My Captain!
Chapter 2: Prerequisites
Chapter 3: Coarse Objectives
Week 2
Chapter 4: Grade Will Reflect
Chapter 5: Coarse Policies
Chapter 6: A Portrait of the Adjunct as a Young Man
Week 3
Chapter 7: Office Hours
Chapter 8: Life, Liberty, and the Pursuit of Copy Credits
Chapter 9: Withdrawal Policy
Week 4
Chapter 10: Absences
Chapter 11: Prof-Reading
Chapter 12: Participation Points
Week 5
Chapter 13: Coarse Descriptions
Chapter 14: Handouts
Chapter 15: Role Call
Week 6
Chapter 16: WAC
Chapter 17: Coarse Requirements
Chapter 18: Assignments
Week 7
Chapter 19: Practice Test
Chapter 20: Errant Nights

The lunatics have taken over the asylum.
— Richard Rowland

Those who can't do, teach.
— Somebody

Introduction to the Class

CHAPTER 1
O Captain! My Captain!

For Berlin Saunders, playing dead came easy. He had been teaching English Composition at the city college in Long Beach for twelve years already and knew better than anyone what faking it was. But today he feared the worst. It was certainly not the most vicious attack he had experienced that day, only the most violent. Barely twenty minutes before the gunman barged into his classroom, he had been upstairs defending himself against a negative performance evaluation given by Harry Crawford—chair of the English Department and author of the self-published, mandatory classroom schlock *Au Revoir, Strunk and White!* Too bad the prick hadn't shown up for the classroom observation today instead of a month ago. Not only that, Saunders was quite possibly giving the best performance of his life right now.

He wondered why, even while lying facedown on the classroom floor, Crawford's evaluation bothered him so much. Shouldn't he, if anything, be thinking of a way out of this? Or was his life flashing before his eyes just a stern reminder it was okay to die? He had been trying to find a way to kill himself all semester, and maybe, just maybe, the gods decided to place matters in someone else's hands. But who better qualified than Saunders himself? He had spent almost the entire semester revising his suicide note (sometimes, he thought, his being a stickler was the only thing that kept him alive), and wasn't about to waste his death on somebody else.

And where did the gunman go? When, if at all, would he be returning? Was it safe yet to open his eyes?

It had been no coincidence that Crawford snubbed Saunders in his evaluation, given their shared history with Kathy Stone, Professor of Women's Studies, and newly deemed co-author of the revised edition of *Au Revoir*. For five years, Kathy had been Saunders's lover. At the end of last semester, their relationship crumbled one drunken night when Saunders admitted to her that not only did he hate "The Yellow Wallpaper," but Charlotte Perkins Gilman was, perhaps, the most hideous-looking woman in American literature. Appalled at the "inappropriateness" of his "misogynistic behavior," and unable to forgive him for it, Kathy threw a glass of wine at his chest, and later sought refuge in Crawford, a man who up until then Saunders believed to be gay.

But as much as he hated to admit it, *Au Revoir* had—at least temporarily—saved him. He had been standing at the front of the classroom, readying himself to give the final lesson of the semester, book-in-hand, when the masked gunman swung open the door and started firing. The shock of being hit made him fall back, but the book stopped the impact of the bullet. It was enough to startle him, but not enough to kill him. At first, he lay there and waited on death. When he failed to feel any pain, he began to realize that he had been spared. The only thing to do was to fake it until he was safe again.

Saunders couldn't help but feel that somehow this was all his fault. Though he couldn't see the gunman's face, he thought he knew for certain who it was. After all, Adam Rowan hadn't shown up for class this morning. Adam was over a decade younger than Saunders, but had struck up a most unlikely bond with him.

In some ways, given the current circumstances, living through this attack might not be the best thing. At least if he died, a chance existed he could be martyred. But in staying alive, nothing could be done about it—he would be chastised for not reporting what the administration would call "warning signs."

Saunders felt the old twitch in his left eye return. It was something he had developed a couple semesters ago. The doctor told him the twitching was stress-related, and gave him a free sample of a medication called *Exstress*, which Saunders hadn't ended up taking, but had noticed a typo on the packaging that said, "designed specifically to help you *relive* stress."

What really got him was he hadn't even been slated to teach this section. Tom Corona had begged him to switch at the last minute so he could do more committee work, something Tom had desperately needed for his CV since he was applying for the full-time tenure-track position in the department this year—a dream Saunders himself once courted, but had recently given up.

"I'm not discouraged," Tom had told him, when he'd heard there'd been over 200 applicants. "I work hard around here."

It was true. Tom had been in the department for only half as long as Saunders, but had gained many more academic accolades in the process—not to mention he was the English Department poster boy, who sucked up to Crawford every chance he got. If there were such a thing as a teacher's *teacher's* pet, it was definitely Tom Corona. He joined every committee, sat through every training workshop, attended the weekly faculty meetings (even though it was not required of adjuncts), and contributed regularly to the discussion thread on the LISTSERV, all in the hope of one day achieving his goal.

But none of this really mattered right now.

Everything had grown still inside the classroom. The screams of Saunders's students had died down and all was silent.

He thought of those movies about inspirational teachers he had come to hate so much. He thought of the end of *Dead Poets Society* when the students stood up on their desks and shouted "O Captain! My Captain!" at Mr. Keating, aka Robin Williams. He wondered what Mr. Keating would've done in his predicament. Would he have whispered "carpe diem" in the ear of each student about to be shot? He wondered what Mr. Keating's performance evaluation would've looked like.

CHAPTER 2
Prerequisites

Faking his death was minor in comparison to the lies Berlin Saunders had been telling all his life. The first **lies** he had ever told were about his father. And the first people, ironically enough, he remembered telling them to were his sympathetic schoolteachers. One story he liked to tell was that his father died in a car accident when his mother was still pregnant with him. Eventually, as he grew older, the lies mutated, and he came up with more imaginative tales to explain his father away, from going missing in the jungles of South Vietnam to living in a witness protection program in Europe. When the truth was, Saunders had merely been the product of a one-night stand.

And if the first lies he ever told were about his father, the biggest lies he ever told were the ones he gave his students on the first day that semester, weeks before the shooter appeared:

Success in any college class is a joint contract between professor and student. By the end of this class, you will gain confidence as both a writer and thinker. You will be able to demonstrate an understanding of the ways that language and communication shape experience, construct meaning, and foster community. The readings have been carefully selected to enhance and excite your curiosities about the nature of human experience. In many ways, writing is an act of discovery. So come prepared to discover!

Admittedly, he had come a bit irritable that day. Though Long

Beach Community College was only one of the two schools he taught part-time at each semester, it was also where he'd met Kathy. And having split up with her recently, and ruining a good shirt in the process, Saunders had approached the spring term on its campus with a malevolence that made him want to bulldoze the Humanities building.

The room he had been given for his first class was even dodgier than usual. Paint was peeling off the walls, ceiling tiles were missing, and a dead cockroach lay on its back in the corner. Having run out of seats, students crowded the aisles, some standing, some cross-legged on the floor. The room stunk and was so hot it felt as if the heater had been on full blast all winter long, trapping the last nervous fart let go during final exams the previous semester.

Saunders made his way down to the front of the class like he did every semester, only to find the chair from his desk missing. He looked around, half-expecting some student to rise and give him back his seat, but none did; they all just stared at him while he set his bag down on top of his desk, and slid the podium—left in the corner—next to it.

His armpits were sweating already. He wasn't sure if it was from the classroom heat or residual from his hangover that morning. Unable to sleep the night before, he had made his way to a bar down the street from his apartment where an old friend worked, and had proceeded to numb himself.

"Anyone know where my chair is?" Saunders mumbled it, kind of joking, kind of humiliated, kind of tired. These were the first words he would speak to his students this semester, and he couldn't help but laugh at the personal irony of the question. *He's off fucking your girlfriend,* he told himself reluctantly. *That's where your "chair" is.*

"I'd hate to think somebody's lying to me so early in the semester," Saunders joked.

The students cared even less than he did about being there. He wondered if this wasn't an act of sabotage, orchestrated by Crawford himself. After all, one of the first things Crawford told him, upon hiring him twelve years ago, was that a good teacher never sits but always stands. *And what would Crawford say about lying down?*

Unable to locate his chair, Saunders unbuckled his leather bag and pulled out his assortment of multi-colored dry erase markers. The first thing he did each semester was write his name, class, and room number on the board, and ask everybody if they were in the right place. Inevitably, somebody wouldn't be. But this time, Saunders felt out of place. Maybe he should've taken the missing chair as an omen and fled the campus. But instead, he looked one more time around the classroom, where he spotted a skinny white male with a crew cut, older than most of the other students, maybe in his late twenties, hunched over, hands in the front pockets of his sweatshirt, looking at the floor.

"Ah-ha," Saunders said, addressing the class. "I think I've found the culprit."

The students turned to look at the young man and he looked back at them, then quickly reached for a camouflage backpack next to him and stood up. Saunders felt guilty for pulling rank and humiliating him in front of the class—especially since the young man probably hadn't even realized it. He tried to make light of the situation, but his mood made everything sound bitter.

"The first rule of this class, ladies and gentlemen," he said, "is to make sure the teacher always has a place to sit."

The students' laughs seemed uncertain. They had not sized-up the kind of teacher he was going to be. He liked their continuing uncertainty, as if it helped him regain control of the situation. In the meantime, the young man, embarrassed, gave Saunders back the chair.

Saunders pulled out the roster and a stack of syllabi from a folder in his bag and set it on the podium.

The young man, not having a seat anymore, seemed confused about where to go and crouched down against the wall next to where he once sat. Saunders felt bad, but knew better than to let down his guard on the first day of class.

"What's your name?" he asked.

After all that fuss about the chair, he had decided to stand at the podium anyway and took the paper clip off the stack of syllabi he was going to pass out.

"Adam," the young man said, as if surprised Saunders asked.

"Adam who?"

"Adam Rowan."

He looked over the roster, running his finger down the list of last names until he found it. He finished calling roll, then distributed the syllabi in each row.

"Adam," he said, handing him the last syllabus, "have you ever told a lie before?"

Concerned, perhaps, as to whether or not a right answer existed and what the consequences of getting it wrong might be, Adam looked around the room then nodded.

"Good," Saunders said. "Then do us the honor. Please read the Course Objectives from page one of the syllabus."

CHAPTER 3
Coarse Objectives

Only two nights before the beginning of the spring semester, Saunders had sat down to update his syllabus, but instead found himself thinking about writing a suicide note. So, he decided to do what any other sensible suicidal English teacher might have: he put his thoughts in writing. Perhaps, by generating ideas for his suicide note, he could better assess (at least according to Diana Hacker's *Rules for Writers* which he kept on his desk) his "specific writing situation." He decided to take the same approach he would with anything else he might write, by first considering his audience, which, of course, depended upon the manner and place in which he killed himself. Since he lived alone, if he were to do it at home, it was likely the first person to discover his body would be someone he probably didn't know, a neighbor or a police officer or a UPS driver (though he doubted he'd be expecting any packages in those final days).

Having spent so many years teaching composition, he knew the importance of getting started early on a draft of his suicide note. He knew it was the last thing anyone would remember him by, and he wanted it to be exceptional. Having decided to do some research, he was left truly disappointed with the caliber of suicide notes he found on the Internet that night, the careless manner in which so many were written: clichéd, purposeless, rife with spelling and grammatical errors, poorly edited, as if the person writing it had waited until they'd already shoved the pills down their throat before jotting down the last trite expressions, which somehow made their suicide more tragic.

Saunders quickly found himself with writer's block.

Who did one address a suicide note to? In his case, there was no particular person he was writing it for, a lost lover (no way would he give Kathy Stone the honor), a child (he had none), a good friend (his only friend had given up his career as a grad student to become a rock star), nor did he want to use the generic and un-engaging "To Whom It May Concern," his standard address anytime a student asked for a letter of recommendation.

To Whom It May Concern:

I am writing with the utmost confidence in recommending Mr. Berlin Saunders to decay and nothingness for the rest of eternity. Mr. Saunders has already proven himself an excellent corpse in life, and it is my belief that he would make an even greater candidate on the other side.

"The key to being a good writer," he told the class every semester, "is not to focus on punctuation and grammar, but on truth-telling."

Of course, who was he kidding? He was much better at correcting punctuation and grammar than he had ever been at telling the truth. He wondered if this writer's block was merely a result of his fear of doing just that. And what came of it the last time he tried being honest? Kathy Stone became co-editor of *Au Revoir*.

Maybe he should just forfeit writing a note altogether. More mystery would surround his death that way. Although, if he did that, any reason he might have for committing suicide would be hijacked. People would begin to fill in the blanks of his mysterious death. He'd be portrayed as just another cynical English teacher who hated Charlotte Perkins Gilman. It dawned on him in the midst of these thoughts that even *she* had committed suicide, sticking to that greatest of all literary traditions next to alcoholism. He wondered what hers and other famous writers' farewell notes must've looked like. He scrolled through his search on "suicide notes," still on the screen, and became distracted by the computer-generated pop-ups that appeared in the right column of his search results:

Suicide Notes at Amazon.com!

Find and Compare Suicide Notes at Smarter.com!

And his favorite:

Suicide Notes Ringtones!

Maybe he was just being too hard on himself. He'd get there. After all, it was only the first time he seriously attempted to write a suicide note. Once he fleshed out his reasons for wanting to die, he would be better able to write the first draft. What was that "specific writing situation" in which he found himself? What was his objective in penning his final message to the world?

When all usefulness is over, when one is assured of an unavoidable and imminent death, it is the simplest of human rights to choose a quick and easy death in place of a slow and horrible one.

Charlotte Perkins Gilman's suicide note.

How could he ever be so eloquent? And though he hated to admit it, he also understood what she meant, even if she was partly alluding to being diagnosed with terminal cancer, her own "specific writing situation."

He had taken pride in all of his achievements in grad school, and had developed the belief that teaching was the noblest of all professions, not to mention the best way to avoid working summers (which wasn't even true for most adjuncts). But at some point, he had lost faith in his profession. And why, for the life of him, should he have any delusions? The note helped him solidify his reason for wanting to commit suicide.

His usefulness had ended.

CHAPTER 4
Grade Will Reflect

Saunders finished the first class session of the spring semester after only twenty minutes, despite the dean's plea in an email to hold students at least half an hour. With time to kill before his next class, and since there wasn't any proper office space for an adjunct to rest his head (besides a couple of desks in the mailroom), he wanted nothing more than to sit in his car and snooze for an hour. Still hungover from the night before, still sweaty despite the January weather, he had taken his blazer off and thrown it over his shoulder as he made his way down through the crowded campus in the direction of his car, when he heard someone calling his name.

"Mr. Saunders!"

From the corner of his eye, he spotted Tina Dees, one hand on her rather wide hip, the other holding her backpack, which is all he had time to see before he swiftly ducked into the food court. He had to act fast before being forced into providing an explanation as to why he denied her request for a grade change last summer.

During this past fall semester, having ignored three voicemail messages from Tina questioning her grade, then denying her official request, he thought it would all end, that she would give up. He didn't have any animosity for Tina, or any of his students, for that matter. In fact, she'd been a pleasure to have in class. But the points just hadn't added up the way she wanted and he thought it a dangerous idea to go back on a decision he'd already made. Something about doing that upset the whole foundation of his principles, the little, at least, that remained intact at the beginning of the semester.

He crossed the food court, which was really just a handful of broken plastic tables and a cafeteria that sold expired bags of potato chips, heat-lamped breakfast burritos, and lukewarm coffee. On the other side, stands had been set up by local vendors to sell cheap jewelry, or the Union Jack, or posters of James Dean, Marilyn Monroe, Barack Obama, Hillary Clinton, Tupac Shakur. Saunders had even bought a framed print of the famous American flag painting by Jasper Johns one semester, discounted at only ten bucks.

The college felt like a goddamned shopping mall during an after-Christmas sale. And truth be told, it wasn't that much different. And if the college was a shopping mall then "English" was the department store he worked for. After all, he still earned an hourly wage, just as he had in the countless retail jobs in college. Every semester he got evaluated anonymously by his students, similar to the "secret shopper" evaluations he received during his time in retail. Like the "secret shopper," each student was expected to respond to a series of comments in which to rate him as "honestly" and "accurately" as possible, using a scale of five to one, in which they could choose from STRONGLY AGREE (5) to STRONGLY DISAGREE (1), or mark NON-APPLICABLE:

The instructor was well prepared for classes and provided clear and accurate information regarding course policies, requirements, grading procedures, and getting shot at.

What was the Rate My Professors website but a glorified consumer report with chili peppers to mark the hotness of each professor? Saunders felt lousy about the results he earned in this category. In all his time teaching, he only ever received one chili pepper, which he gave to himself. No one in the Humanities division of the college racked up much zest in that category, especially not the women.

"Do you think good-looking women go to grad school?" his colleague Ray Zapata warned him truthfully once when he expressed the hope of meeting one. "You might as well have joined the Army."

Yes, the Humanities division of the college wasn't exactly the Miss America pageant. Even Kathy had been nothing to cancel class over—she had nice legs, but her nose protruded too far from her face and over the years, her arms had gotten flabby. But unlike so many of her colleagues in the Women's Studies department, she had stood out, a radical of sorts, who still wanted to be desired by the opposite sex. She even wore skirts occasionally and carried a mirror in her purse.

Saunders felt ashamed of his shallowness, especially given that, bald and beer-bellied, he was no heartthrob either. He even felt somehow responsible for inspiring her revolt during the last few years they were together. He couldn't deny the fact that his attraction to her had been thwarted by knowing she hadn't received a single chili pepper on Rate My Professors. Then again, *she* left *him*. But when they had met that day in the mailroom, they had immediately connected with each other—she with her white scarf with black polka dots (which only later did he learn were not polka dots, but little black hearts) and a copy of Djuna Barnes *Nightwood* in her hand, and he with his brown corduroy blazer—elbow patches and all—flipping through the latest New Directions catalogue left in his box.

"Hey, Mr. Saunders!"

There was Tina again, heading his way. He ducked behind the library, trying to lose her.

Customer Service, indeed, this great American tradition of education, and not only was he a product of it himself, he was now one of its products. Both education and retail abided by the same principle: the customer's always right. Students weren't just students, but patrons, who expected to get the most for their money, usually in the form of a good grade. And he was currently being chased by an unsatisfied customer.

Memos sent on the first day of class advised adjuncts not to add any new students for at least a week as a way of discouraging them from "shopping" for the right teacher. And really, who could blame them? The right teacher could be the difference between failing and getting a passing grade. And if, like all good customers, they weren't happy with the service they received, they would just complain about it or take it to a higher authority until they got what they wanted.

"Mr. Saunders! Are you ignoring me?"

The customer's always right. And now you will pay the consequences.

He turned one more corner around the planetarium, (built

sometime in the late sixties, when people still cared about stargazing, and not of the celebrity kind), reached into his pocket and pulled out his phone, pretending to call somebody. He braved a look and seemed to have lost her. Though he couldn't be sure yet, he began talking into the phone as if somebody were telling him something important over the receiver, when he spotted Adam Rowan, setting his camouflaged backpack down on a bench next to a tree by the planetarium, watching the whole thing.

Rarely did he know a student by name the first day of class, but given the charade of finding his chair that morning, Rowan's name was ingrained in his psyche.

It was humiliating to think Rowan had witnessed him running away from another student. Then again, what did it really matter? Saunders often thought students noticed things they didn't.

Rowan, wearing earbuds, pretended not to notice Saunders. Why feel anxiety? He would probably drop the course by the end of the week if he even showed up for the next class at all. Anyway, he was probably more humiliated to see Saunders, who had just berated him in front of everyone that morning.

Saunders looked behind Rowan and saw a squirrel running up the branch of a tree. At least it wasn't a rabbit. The whole campus was littered with them now. About four years ago, some hippie biology teacher decided it'd be a good idea to let a bunch of homeless rabbits inherit the grassy knolls and start leaving shit pellets all over the campus.

Having taken a moment to catch his breath after fleeing from Tina Dees, but intent on getting to his car as quickly as possible,

Saunders figured, to save face, he should at least say something to Rowan who he was sure had witnessed his odd behavior. He pulled a smoke out from his blazer pocket when he saw a lighter and pack of cigarettes by Adam's side.

"Can I borrow your fire?" he said.

On a scale of five to one, in which Adam Rowan could choose from STRONGLY AGREE (5) to STRONGLY DISAGREE (1), he had chosen to mark NON-APPLICABLE. He simply nodded at Saunders and handed him the lighter, unveiling very little expression.

"Thanks," Saunders said, then sputtered off something about being late, which was a lie, of course, before walking away.

Besides, customers didn't care about the moral accountability of their service providers, as long as they got what they wanted.

He wondered if he'd ever get to take that nap in his car before his next class started. It seemed so inevitable only a few minutes ago as he made his way through the campus. But soon enough, that question was answered, when once again somebody shouted his name. This time, it wasn't Tina Dees, however; it was Harry Crawford.

CHAPTER 5
Coarse Policies

The first run-in between Saunders and Crawford since the breakup with Kathy seemed relatively civilized, considering. All winter long, Saunders had been confronted with the inevitability of this moment. And yet, none of the open and deliberate violence, which over the break seemed like the most soothing solution, had occurred. He was going to commit suicide anyhow, so what did he have to lose? The dead didn't need jobs. Instead, he took the more dignified approach, so as to not make it so easy for Crawford. But in reality, Crawford had already lost by gaining Kathy, and, if anything, he should be pitied. Or was it the other way? When Saunders was truly honest with himself, could he admit that Kathy had stained much more than his shirt?

Either way, as they stood in front of each other in the quad that day, the sun directly over the planetarium, sweat beads bursting out of the pores beneath Saunders's eyelashes while students, teachers, and even a military recruiter passed by, there had been no open and deliberate violence like he imagined.

Where's the rage? As he shook Crawford's limp-dick hand, he recalled a protest sign posted on a window of the City Lights bookstore, when he and Kathy had driven up to San Francisco for the weekend last summer.

Saunders kept looking around him, any minute expecting Tina Dees to catch up and sink him for good, as much as he might've welcomed the distraction. He blew smoke out of his mouth, then flicked the burning cherry off his cigarette.

"I thought I might catch you out here," Crawford said, pushing his prescription Ray-Bans up on his nose, which made Saunders think how nice it must be to have vision insurance. "How's your first day back, Berlin?"

He put a hand on Saunders's shoulder, as if he hadn't been fucking his ex-girlfriend.

"No complaints," Saunders said, feeling his shoulder tighten. Why such a banal response? He felt like a traitor to himself. He knew a trap was being set, and just wanted to escape from it as quickly as possible.

"Perf," Crawford said. "I'm looking forward to evaluating you this semester."

Perf?

"Not sure exactly when," Crawford continued. "I'll just pop in for twenty minutes or so one day. Don't sweat it. Don't do anything special."

That last line was Crawford's catch phrase. His policy was that he didn't like members of the faculty knowing when he was coming to evaluate them because he preferred they didn't prepare anything "special" for his visit. *Like an improvised explosive device?*

"Just procedure," he said, "that's all. You're a seasoned vet. You know how it goes."

Crawford smiled at Saunders. He looked like a middle-aged man posing as an eighties teenager. He even wore a silver brooch.

The eighties were back, but not *that* back. How, he wondered, could Kathy let him leave the house that way? Then again, he didn't really want to think that much about them living together. Did he wear that brooch when they had sex?

"Good news," Crawford said. "Got an order from a prof over at Berkeley says he's gonna use *Au Revoir* in his class."

He probably wears a brooch too.

"It's makin' its way," Crawford said, "which should benefit the whole department."

Crawford reached his hand into his blazer pocket and pulled out a folded copy of the English Department class schedule, then ran his finger down the side of it, letting it linger not too far from the bottom.

"Which reminds me…," he said, "you get that email from the dean about keeping your classes at least half an hour on the first day?"

Saunders tried to do the math between how much time had passed from when he first let the class out and running into Crawford.

"Not sure," he said to Crawford, lying. "But I'll make sure I do that."

Crawford took Saunders's hand and shook it again.

"Really good to see you, Berlin," he said, still gripping it. Saunders wondered how hard he'd have to squeeze Crawford's hand to break at least his pinky.

Just as they were about to depart, Crawford turned back.

"Oh, and one other thing," he said. "Probably not a good idea to be smoking on campus anyway, but remember you need to be twenty-five feet away from all buildings."

Saunders looked for his watch. He kept forgetting how three weeks before he had thrown it against a wall after Kathy, out of the blue, emailed him one night asking if he'd proofread an essay she wrote: *I know this might seem awkward, but you always had such good insight.* The glass was busted and the secondhand crippled so that it permanently stuck at the half-hour mark.

He thought of a watch he once saw in a catalogue, that had a mirror as the face, and the shorthand said, "Remember," while the longhand said, "You will die." It made him feel better to think about that.

CHAPTER 6
A PORTRAIT OF THE ADJUNCT AS A YOUNG MAN

The truth is if it weren't for Adam Rowan, it would've been something else that forced the end of Saunders's teaching career. For it had been coming a long time now, and he hadn't felt this phony since his mother had taken him to see a Hollywood agent at the age of nine.

Sometime during the early nineteen-eighties, his mother went from being a hippie mom to a celebrity-obsessed wannabe stage mom. Saunders and his mother had moved in with his grandparents in Anaheim. And his mother—unemployed, with no boyfriend—had snapped a few Polaroids of him and sent them to a half-dozen or so Hollywood agents, with one enthusiastically responding that with his freckled-face, blue eyes, and light brown curly hair, Saunders bore the look of an "all-American boy."

"It's true," his mother told him in the parking lot that day, brushing his bangs out of his eyes before going in to meet the agent for an interview. "My handsome, all-American boy!"

Later, of course, he would laugh at the stereotypes that made him "all-American." It wouldn't be until he met Rowan that he realized what truly made him "all-American" was not his blue eyes or freckled-face, but that he was fatherless.

The introspection still years in the distance, Saunders's mother had asked him to smile that afternoon so she could inspect his teeth, to make sure he didn't need to use the toothbrush she packed in a Ziploc baggie before they got out of the car and went up to the agent's office. He wanted to turn back, go ride his bike around his neighborhood, but instead found himself dragged into an elevator of a high rise somewhere off Sunset Boulevard, his face growing increasingly red with each passing floor.

"Try this," the agent said, handing him a side for a milk commercial once they settled into her office. She was a plump woman, who wore lots of bracelets around her wrists that clanked when she moved her chubby hands. "Let's see how it goes."

He glanced up at his mother as if to ask if he really had to read the lines out loud, but the look she gave him said perk up or pay the price.

"Milk," he said, staring down at the paper, and pretending to take a sip from a non-existent glass. "It does a body …."

He paused. He couldn't complete the last line. The agent sighed, waiting for him, mouthing the word "good."

"Go on," she finally told him.

"I can't," Saunders said, dropping his hands so that the side brushed the leg of his chair.

"Why can't you?" his mother said, looking down at him.

He sat quiet for a moment, weighing his options.

"It's not right," he said.

"What do you mean it's not right?" his mother said.

"Milk does a body *well*," he said.

Disappointed her son would never be a famous child actor, his mother never pushed him to do anything else, and by the time he was a junior in high school, his grade point average was so bad,

Saunders was all but certain he wouldn't go to college.

It wasn't so much a dislike for school that made him a bad student, but rather a loss of confidence. This would change his senior year, when his twelfth grade English teacher, Ms. Salazar, who had the tiniest waist he had ever seen, would read his paper on Nathaniel Hawthorne's *The Scarlet Letter* to the class.

"'If anything,'" she read, quoting his paper, "'the 'A' on Hester's shirt must stand for America.' Now isn't that insightful, Berlin."

Her appraisal of his work (along with the massive crush he had developed on her), left him with a passion to read everything. After that, he stayed in his room every night with candles lit, ingesting stories by nineteenth century American Gothic writers like Poe, as well as other American writers like Hawthorne, Thoreau, Herman Melville, Stephen Crane, and even Ambrose Bierce, as he dreamt of becoming the world's greatest writer.

He yearned to live an authentic life, a life of poetry and compassion. He wanted to "sing" himself (having been inspired by Walt Whitman's *Leaves of Grass* by this time), to travel and ignite the world, to drink and have adulterous affairs with exotic women.

Eventually, at eighteen, he lost his virginity to his first girlfriend (who used to irritate him by pronouncing "picture" as "pitcher"). And as he moved through his early twenties, spending time getting the most useless degree he could possibly think of—an M.F.A. in poetry—the idealism of his youth began to fade. The critical nature of the workshop left him with nothing but doubt about his talent, and gave him the fear of what the hell else to do with his life. He became too self-conscious to write anything creative again, realizing he'd live less like a Whitman poem and more like Thoreau's man of quiet desperation. So by the time he finished grad school, and crashed on the comfortable cushion of academia, he had already conformed to all the policies and adopted the same ideologies as most of his peers: those safe, left-leaning, condescending, uninspired, dimwits of drudgery, who loved to flout their excellence to anyone who would listen. And for the next twelve years, this is how he stayed.

But had he always felt this way? Hadn't he once believed he could make a difference in his students' lives? When had he become just an actor, forfeiting the desires and cravings of his idealism to teach others how to write a thesis statement? And what happened to his own life's thesis? When had it become so insupportable?

CHAPTER 7
Office Hours

That first night of the spring semester, after class, Saunders returned to 3636, the same bar responsible for his hangover—a mildew-scented dive with most of the felt worn off the only pool table and lacking a door on the men's restroom. With him was the recent Grossman translation of *Don Quixote*, which he picked up shortly after Christmas. He was supposed to read all 450 pages of Part I for his book club meeting the following Sunday. George Glazer, a faculty member in the Art History Department, who introduced himself to Saunders one morning last year in the Humanities Division mailroom, had been pestering him to join a book club that he and his wife, a high school English teacher, created. For the first time, Saunders agreed to attend after almost a year of being invited, mostly because he always wanted to read *Don Quixote*, but also because it'd be the first opportunity to prowl since the breakup with Kathy. Despite the dim odds of meeting an attractive woman at an event like that, and against his better judgment about even wanting to, he could only hope Glazer's wife had friends.

Saunders doubted he'd get any reading done at the bar that evening, but felt comfortable having the book in front of him, a security blanket he could always pull over his head if, god forbid, anyone decided to talk to him. He had been reluctant to start the novel at all given that he tended to be the type who had to finish a book, even if it meant postponing a pending suicide. Even if he completed the first part by Sunday night, he knew it could take months to get through the whole thing. George Glazer split the reading of the book in two and a discussion of the second half would come later in the semester.

An old roommate of his, Phil, worked four nights a week at the bar, earned more money than Saunders did, and even got to break up a fight now and then. The closest Saunders ever got to a fight was between two female students arguing about the promises their babies' daddies were making from prison. Phil looked like a cross between Brad Pitt and Kid Rock and was probably the only guy Saunders knew who still had a ponytail. He usually came in around six, but when Saunders got there about a quarter 'til, he was already behind the bar. The place was empty, generally a good sign because it meant he could hole up in his favorite corner seat on the far left and nobody would bother him. But a bored Phil meant more danger, as he liked to serve up more shots when there was nothing better to do—none of which he required Saunders to pay for. What did it matter anyway? Though he had never been a heavy drinker, since his decision to commit suicide only two nights before, Saunders formed a new union with alcohol, bent on the idea of annihilating himself with it. Of course, his head pounding the way it was, he wondered if it might just be easier to blow his brains out.

"Mr. Professor," Phil said, who was at the other end of the bar soaking glasses in dirty soap water when he sat down. He wiped his hands on a rag in his back pocket before greeting him. "Glad to see you're alive today."

"*Alive* is relative," Saunders said, shaking his hand. "Give me a Bloody Mary and I'll try not to blame you for getting me so fucked up last night."

Phil smiled. On television at the other end of the bar, a news channel was gearing up for the State of the Union address.

Saunders's Bloody Mary was waiting for him when he returned from a trip to the bathroom and Phil poured him a shot of Jägermeister, German for the sickest fucking shit he had ever tasted.

"To your mother's children."

Phil raised his glass and toasted Saunders, who had never been very good at taking shots. He held the Jägermeister inside his mouth for a long time before swallowing, almost hurling all over the bar. Phil placed a water in front of him, which he was thankful for, and sipped it quickly before switching back to his drink. It'd be a long and difficult task boozing himself to death if he kept taking shots like a sissy. He wouldn't, at least, be able to hold his brains in his mouth.

Once the booze settled in, though, he began to relax, and not surprisingly, felt much better. He bought a new pack of cigarettes out of a machine next to the jukebox, and packed them on the edge of the bar before going outside to smoke.

When he came back, Phil was fiddling with a crossword puzzle from a book he kept behind the cash register and had nearly filled up.

"Ok, answer me this question, Mr. Professor," Phil said, looking down at the book.

Saunders wasn't any good at crosswords. It was the English

teacher in him. The abbreviations and odd spellings always threw him off.

"I don't do crosswords," he said to Phil.

Saunders figured anything Phil didn't know he wasn't gonna know either. Phil was smarter and better read than most of the academics he worked with, but dropped out of college with only twelve units to go on an Anthropology bachelor's. He opted for field work behind a bar instead, which, come to think of it, probably produced much more interesting results than studying some nomad tribe in Africa.

Phil himself was a nomad: he'd managed to live outside of the culture for a while now, with no driver's license, no bank account, no woman, no political party affiliation, and no cell phone. All the money he earned at the bar was in tips and a minor payout for his hourly wages. For all intents and purposes, Phil didn't exist, which Saunders had begun to find quite appealing.

"It's five letters," Phil said. "Who is that 'other' famous Thomas of 1776?"

He might know this one, if his still-lingering hangover didn't slow him down too much. The implication of the "other" Thomas already excluded Jefferson, and the only other Thomas he could think of, Thomas Edison, was much later. Just because he taught great American essays in his English composition class didn't mean he knew his American history all that well.

A petite, attractive Gwen Stefani-looking chick (not his type), with a sleeve of tattoos and pink hair, walked in, talking on her cell phone. She couldn't have been any more than 22, 23. She slumped down on the stool next to Saunders and smiled at Phil, who gave her a little wave… leaving Saunders to wonder if he was fucking her.

"We have rock star professions," Phil told him later, never humble about the number of women he'd slept with from the bar. "Don't act like it doesn't happen to you, Mr. Professor."

Of course, Saunders pretended it did. But the truth was, in over a decade of teaching, it hadn't happened once. And despite the constant inquiry by male friends about the myth of female students wanting to sleep with their professors, and despite the dozens of Philip Roth novels he'd read in anticipation, Saunders only ever had one student come on to him in an English 100 class for a passing grade, and she was a cracked-out, middle-aged woman who used a walker to get around.

"Come on, Professor," she told him in front of the other students, "let me take care of you after class."

"It's a name so common I'm missin' it," Phil said, still searching for that answer.

"Think harder, man," Saunders said.

Phil placed the book on top of the bar and slid it over in front of Gwen Stefani, who, still on the phone, looked at the question, then replied with a shrug.

"Paine," Saunders said. "Thomas Paine!"

The word "common" tipped him off, and made him think of Paine's famous pamphlet, which he remembered studying way back in one of his early American literature classes. Phil high-fived him and poured them two more shots of Jäger and a third shot, which he placed in front of the girl.

"Hold on a minute," she said to whoever was on the other end of the phone. "I gotta take a shot with Phil and some nerd."

It was true, of course, he was a nerd. But he tended to overlook how others might see him—particularly in a bar where everyone generally only saw you as a drunk or an asshole, or usually both.

"Not bad, Mr. Professor," Phil said. "Let's see if you know this Revolutionary War one."

Saunders shook his head.

"That was beginner's luck. I don't know shit about the Revolutionary War."

"What famous American patriot said, 'Give me liberty or give me death'?"

"No fucking clue."

"Me neither," Phil said.

All three of them held up their shots.

"Give me Jäger or give me death," Phil said.

He clicked his shot glass too hard against Saunders's so that the Jäger spilled over the rim and onto the bar, while the president of the United States, delivering his State of the Union Address in the Chamber of the House of Representatives, said over the television, "In neighborhoods across our country, there are boys and girls with dreams—and a decent education is their only hope of achieving them."

CHAPTER 8
Life, Liberty, and the Pursuit of Copy Credits

On the second day of the spring semester, the English Department faculty had been required to conduct what was called a "writing diagnostic" with all the students in their composition courses, designed to check for any signs and symptoms of deficiency in a student's writing. Saunders found the medical terminology to be appropriate since many teachers in the department already thought of their students as ill. After all, it was the teacher's job to interpret the results of the exam before providing them with care.

In some cases, if further treatment was necessary, beyond the general practice, teachers had to resort to the specialists in the writing "lab," which the college established on campus to further assist those with the severest conditions. What the terminology amounted to, ultimately, was a belief in two things: writing was an exact science in which any deficiencies could be cured with one composition class (which, of course, they couldn't), and, secondly, that the English Department was just a great big hospital and it was no coincidence that the majority of people working for it were called doctors. If Saunders followed that metaphor, then his students this semester were about to be victims of malpractice. He had already made up his mind not to "diagnose" a single page of their writing samples.

Would a doctor commit suicide in the midst of treating his patients? A dentist certainly would. He laughed as he drove around in circles trying to find a space in the staff parking lot, wondering why dentists, of all people, had the highest suicide rate.

There had been heavier than usual traffic that morning, and in a rush, he almost hit a suicidal rabbit in the middle of the parking lot, having to slam on his brakes when the pudgy white critter hopped out in front of his car.

Feeling the pressure of time, he parked in a red space marked RESERVED. It was risky. The spaces were designated for administrators only, but tons were available. He'd be damned if he was going to let Crawford have anything on him. The last thing he needed was his students stopping by the English Department to inquire about the whereabouts of their professor.

Inspired by last night's crossword puzzle, he had decided to make copies of *The Declaration of Independence* and have his students write a response. But after making only 10 copies in the faculty copy room, the machine shut off.

"Didn't you see the sign?" said Joanne, the department secretary.

The whole department was afraid of Joanne, but Saunders had always gotten along with her. She had short, spiky hair and a large disco ball over her desk, so light bubbles turned above her head all day while she worked and blasted techno music.

ATTENTION ALL FACULTY:

DUE TO BUDGET CUTS WE ARE RATIONING COPIES AND YOU WILL ONLY BE ALLOTTED 10 TOTAL COPY CREDITS FROM THE DEPARTMENT MACHINE THIS SEMESTER. SO PLEASE ARRANGE TO HAVE THEM MADE ELSEWHERE.

SORRY FOR THE INCONVENIENCE.

"What's the point?" Saunders asked.

"I don't make the rules," she said. "I just make signs about them."

So instead, he put the deceptively simple prompt on the board.

Write your autobiography in 100 words.

"Do you care if it's in pencil?" asked a student whose name he had yet to learn.

"I don't care if it's in Japanese," Saunders said, creating a few laughs.

"How long is 100 words?" somebody else asked.

He gave them about twenty minutes at the end of class to do the sample. The majority of his students finished quickly, turned in their papers, and got out of there. Only two students hadn't turned in their work by the end, a rather ugly blonde girl who looked like she was recopying her original draft to make it as neat as possible, and Adam Rowan, who kept neurotically scratching out the first few lines of his paper and rewriting them.

"I'm stuck," he told Saunders.

Tell me about it. A terror fell over Saunders at the possibility that the rest of his life was going to feel just as this student's did at that moment. And if he were ever going to do this thing, to cease living, how could he continue to treat his "patients" … especially with a prognosis so much worse than theirs?

"You're probably over-thinking it," Saunders said, knowing this problem well. He didn't want to have that conversation, just wanted to get out of the classroom. Hadn't they been sitting there for long enough already? Not only that, he was hungry and had limited time before his next class to eat. But then he looked at the ugly young girl recopying her paper, trying to make it as perfect as possible, and wondered if she'd ever even kissed a boy. Eighteen years old. Was she a virgin still? Would she ever find a man to tolerate that face? Men were assholes. It was true. Himself included. Suddenly, Saunders filled with empathy for all of humanity. That only lasted a minute.

"Listen," he said, "I'm sure what you both have is fine. Just give me what you've got."

The blonde girl stood up, meticulously tearing her paper from a spiral notebook. Saunders watched as she stuffed her notebook into her backpack, threw it over her shoulder, walked up to the desk, turned in her paper, and left.

Finally, a frustrated Adam put his pen down and asked Saunders if it'd be all right if he finished it at home.

"Fine," Saunders told him. "Email me something by the end of the day."

"You're probably not gonna like it anyway," Adam said.

I'm probably not even going to read it, Saunders wanted to tell him, but instead, just smiled and collected his bag.

What did he care? Despite what he told himself, he just couldn't be the bad guy. Everyone deserves a second chance.

Unless they park in an administrator's spot, of course. He plucked the ticket off his windshield just as he heard the screeching of brakes, and looked up in time to see a red Toyota Prius with brand new plates go skidding through the parking lot, ending in a loud thump. Saunders knew exactly what the thump was. Goddamn rabbits. The only thing that wasn't rationed on this campus.

CHAPTER 9
Withdrawal Policy

That night, just to feel inspired, Saunders watched a documentary on Netflix about people committing suicide off the Golden Gate Bridge. One of the saddest parts of the film was when a passerby saved a young girl from jumping, after she'd climbed over the railing right in front of him. Maybe she really wanted to be saved, but he felt sorry for the girl when the man lifted her up by her jacket and back over against her will. What right did he have to make her continue living?

After watching the documentary, he logged onto Facebook, and saw he had a message from his best friend Will, who he hadn't seen since he'd gotten a big break over a year ago, touring the world and playing guitar in a recently reformed nineties rock band.

Hey King, the message said, *How's the grind? Can't say I miss it man! Being on a rock tour may not be as epic as one would think, but I certainly don't miss grading those fucking composition papers! See you soon! Send my love to Kathy. P.S. I met Pete Townshend last night. Nice guy!*

He'd met Will in community college, before they'd gone their separate ways, Saunders to get his M.F.A. and Will to get his Ph.D. in English. Saunders liked to joke that Will had done everything in reverse—becoming a rock star had ended up being his backup plan. If only he'd learned to play an instrument himself. He'd been too depressed to answer Will's messages lately, not wanting to tell him about Kathy.

Saunders changed his profile picture to a foggy Golden Gate Bridge on what looked like an eerie San Francisco morning. He opened up his vintage black leather school bag, which had been a hand-me-down from an old professor he worked for in grad school. To Saunders, it was just a piece of shit with holes in the bottom of the front pockets through which he was constantly losing pencils, pens, dry erase markers, and paper clips. But Tom Corona, that kiss ass, sure loved it. And he felt obliged to tell him as much every time Saunders ran into him on campus. "Have I mentioned it today, Saunders?" Maybe he'd leave it for Tom when he killed himself. Yes, he thought, he would—which meant not only did he need to write a suicide note, but he also needed to make a will.

Saunders hadn't cleared out the bag since last semester. He grabbed a couple of old folders to dump in his plastic blue wastebasket under his desk, and also grabbed the stack of writing samples from that day and stuffed them down in the trash. How many years had he wasted reading all of them so diligently? The diagnostic was supposed to be a way to get to know his students and to evaluate their writing skills. How he used to believe it all mattered so much—that he could actually see progress in his students. He'd even grouped them together from strongest writers to weakest and made sure to pair them up for any activities in the semester. How he used to care.

Still, he felt bad about throwing away the writing samples… to ignore this small expression of his students. True they received no real credit for writing them, but there were thirty-five individual voices in there, even if they mostly sounded the same. They were so young, but most were dealing with worse struggles than he had ever known. After all, if he were honest, he hadn't really struggled much compared to others. Most of his struggles had been self-imposed. Some of his students were returning adults who had children, careers, or found themselves unemployed in the slumping economy, hoping to better themselves. What bad luck to wind up with him as their professor. Even if he planned on making this his last semester, he owed them something. He owed them at the very least a glance at their little inarticulate attempts to explain who they were.

He pulled the pile of papers back out of the trash and started reading. Page after page, they described themselves as dedicated, hard-working, full of hope. How could he blame them? Or worse, tell them there wasn't much hope? Did he really believe that?

He moved quickly through the pile as each one began sounding the same. His empathy faded after thirty pages of cliché upon cliché, until he once again felt relieved to find himself comfortably hopeless again. Most of them would not achieve their dreams. Most of them would end up doing a job they hated or hating the career they chose. Most of them would end up divorced, lonely, hated by their children, or childless. Most of them would lie to themselves sometime around the age of forty that their lives were worth living.

There was one writing sample he'd almost forgotten about. And just when he'd resolved himself to never read another one, he checked his email. "You're probably not going to like it," Adam had said in class. Saunders didn't doubt that given the evidence, but just as he was about to right-click and delete the email, curiosity got the best of him, and he opened up the attachment.

If I were to sum up who I am in 100 words, it would be that I am a man who has big plans. A man who seeks justice in this world. A true patriot who loves his country, but can't always trust his government. A societal leper living on the radical fringe surrounded by liberal elitist sheep. A veteran and concerned citizen ready to defend his freedoms as established by the Constitution of this great country, whether that be in his right to own a gun or the right to make his own choices.

The last thing Saunders needed was some right-wing nutjob in his classroom disagreeing with all his liberal viewpoints. All he wanted was an easy semester before he let himself out for a permanent summer break. And yet, he couldn't help but feel the slightest bit jealous—Adam stood for something, didn't he? Saunders had failed to do this for years. Saunders knew nothing about guns and as far as he was concerned, the country could do without them. But how would he know? He'd never shot one, had he? He'd never even shot a *BB* gun. Hell, growing up with a single mother he'd never even fished. Or gone camping. Never been much of a man at all really. Wasn't even handy at anything either. This used to bother Kathy despite her so-called progressive views about gender. She used to get frustrated by his inability to fix things. "Let me do it," she'd say to him, pushing him out of the way of whatever task happened to be at hand. Kathy's father worked as an electrician all his life and had taught his daughter the ins and outs of living in this world. Saunders was no idiot though and it used to bother him whenever Kathy butted in on his attempts at fixing a door hinge or a stuck window, or lighting the burnt-out pilot light in the heater. He couldn't win. When he was too masculine, she'd criticize him as insensitive; when he was too feminine, she loved to humiliate him. But like the folders left in his bag from last semester, this was the past now. There was nothing left to fix.

CHAPTER 10
ABSENCES

At the next class session, when Adam Rowan didn't show up, Saunders thought he had changed his mind and dropped the class. He felt relieved of the burden of having to face this young man. The last thing he needed was a student who cared and wanted to change the world, or worse, a right-wing student who cared and wanted to change the world.

The third day of class was when he usually gave his one big inspirational speech of the semester. His chance to pump his students up about the importance of writing. For so long, he had sincerely believed it. Writing could liberate them from the prisons of consumer culture and help them in their everyday lives. Passion was the best method of teaching and he had put everything into it.

"Language is your birthright!" he'd shout at the class with his fist clenched around his dry erase marker after he'd written this on the board.

But after twelve years of trying, his fist came down. He just didn't give a damn. And because of this, neither did his students.

He was three-fourths through his third day lecture on the writing process. He always expected one of his students to call bullshit, but they never did. When he'd first begun to teach, dissent had been one of his fears. How would he handle it? But dissent never arrived.

And then Adam Rowan showed up, accidently letting the classroom door slam behind him, disrupting Saunders's lecture.

He hadn't dropped. He was just late. Very late.

Saunders's left eye began to twitch as Adam made his way along the back row of the class, clutching his camouflaged backpack. Saunders continued with his lecture.

"We write to express ourselves, we write to inform others, we write even as a form of therapy…"

His lecturing was as automatic as driving these days. Usually by the end of class, he had no memory of saying anything.

Then a hand went up. An important point to make at last? A challenge? Some insightful epiphany he had inspired on only the third day of class?

Since he didn't know his students' names yet, he pointed to the girl who'd raised her hand. She seemed indescribable as they all did the first weeks, just faces, just bodies in desks, just blurs: white, black, Asian, fat, thin, pretty, ugly. Sometimes he never learned their names at all, never found one thing to remember them by. It was like the high school people that had begun to contact him on Facebook, names and faces he couldn't remember.

"May I use the restroom?" the girl said. Some of the other students laughed.

"This is college," Saunders told the girl. "You don't need a hall pass."

The students laughed again as the faceless girl got up and rushed out of the class.

"Okay," Saunders said, "so, where were we?"

They were nowhere. That's where they were. And soon enough they were out of time. They were near the end of the class and Saunders excused them five minutes early, Harry Crawford be damned.

As the students filed out, Adam Rowan approached him.

"Sorry I was so late, professor," he said. "Won't happen again. Traffic was hell."

"It's only the second week of class," Saunders said. "I guess I'll cut you some slack."

After all, soldier, this isn't boot camp.

"Glad I caught the tail end of your lecture though," Adam said. "Great stuff about writing having therapeutic value. But do you really think it can save the world?"

Had he said this?

"Writing's hard work," Saunders said. "But it has its rewards."

"Sticks and stones," Adam said, smiling. "That's what I always say."

At one point in his career, Saunders would have felt defensive and argued with him. All the greatest revolutions had been sparked by words. Martin Luther King. The American Revolution. Gandhi.

"Someone's still got to fire the first shot, you know what I mean?" said Adam.

Maybe so, but violence never solved anything. Direct action only mattered when backed up with substance, which usually relied on words. Otherwise, it was pointless.

"Did you get a chance to read my response?" Adam asked Saunders.

"It was interesting," Saunders said, resorting to the emptiest word in the English language. A word he banned from use in his class during previous semesters for its utter inability to commit to saying anything. "A bit conspiratorial for my taste."

Adam smiled.

"Don't worry," he said. "None of my professors ever agree with me."

Meanwhile, the girl who had gone to the bathroom was back, surprised to find the classroom emptied out.

"Did I miss anything important?" she asked.

"It's all important," Adam said, though Saunders was already shaking his head no.

She picked up her stuff and walked out with Adam, leaving Saunders to himself. He erased the board, packed up his stuff, locked the classroom door, then headed to his car.

Outside it started to rain, and having used his windshield wipers so infrequently, he noticed they could hardly do their job anymore, sliced up by the crack in his windshield that went clear across the front window. For six months, Kathy hounded him to get it fixed.

"But it doesn't bother me," he told her one day when they were carpooling home from work.

"Things used to bother you," she came back at him.

CHAPTER 11
Prof-Reading

"Caught a couple live ones already," Tom Corona said. "Can you believe it?"

Saunders was in the mailroom cleaning out his box when Tom proudly told him he'd caught some plagiarizers. If there was one thing that put a firecracker under the dull sagging khaki asses of English teachers the most, it was finding out one of their eighteen-year-old students cheated.

"Good thing for Copycat," Tom Corona said.

Copycat.com was a system established for faculty members to catch plagiarizers. Teachers across the country had begun to use it in their classrooms. The concept was simple: any student work that got turned in would be run through a computer program that tried to match it with any known writing available on the web. More and more teachers made their students turn in all of their work through this system, including Tom.

"Two plagiarizers so early this semester. Little cheaters can't be trusted."

The year before there had been a departmental request to make use of this system, but Saunders refused to sign up for any of the training courses they offered on campus.

"I don't know," he said. "I'm just not into accusing my students before they've done anything wrong."

"How noble of you," Tom told him. "But they're all guilty of something. No one's going to pull the wool over my eyes. It's just a screener."

Saunders noted Tom's use of a cliché without irony. *Pull the wool.*

"Why did it have to be wool anyway?"

"You don't know why?" Tom said. "Because in the old days when men wore wigs, you could pull their wigs over their eyes as an insult."

And how were his students really any different from him? How were their little lies different from the daily little lies he told them? Really, the whole education system was just one large cesspool of liars: students lying to teachers, teachers lying to students, teachers lying to teachers, students lying to students, administrators lying to teachers, the government lying to the administrators, the government lying to teachers, the government lying to students. What differentiated the act of plagiarism from any other of the countless lies being spun around the nation? Didn't plagiarism equal patriotism? Wasn't it the American way to copy somebody else's work? Hadn't Thomas Jefferson been accused of plagiarizing much of *The Declaration of Independence* from John Locke? Or had he just made that up?

"Besides," Tom said, "it's another thing to add to my résumé. It cost the department $12,000 just to have the account. They want us using it."

As that was said they both heard a loud snore coming from a fat forty-something faculty member, wearing a suit and tie, who had his head down on the table next to the copy machine.

Saunders emptied out the pile of memos in his box. Every semester, the department usually left dry erase markers in each adjunct's box, but he didn't get any this semester. He felt tempted to ask Tom if he had somehow been cheated of his dry erase markers as one more plot of Harry Crawford's, but didn't trust him enough to explain his suspicions. Without even looking, he tossed the pile of papers in the trashcan by the mailboxes.

"I have a student who cares," Saunders said.

"Oh Christ. Why?" Tom said.

"Right-wing, gun-loving type," Saunders said.

"It's always those guys."

"He was even worried about his writing sample."

"What?" Tom said. "Yeah, he cares way too much. Watch out for that one. Probably a bit nutty. Speaking of which, you gonna volunteer for the active shooter drill in a few weeks?"

Saunders had no idea what he was talking about.

"What drill?"

"The active shooter drill," Tom said. "Sign-ups are right now. Didn't you get the email?"

"What are *you* gonna do?"

"I guess I'll be a simulated teacher or something," Tom said. "You know me—I'm just always trying to score brownie points. But I think this will actually be fun. There's going to be mock gunfire and everything."

"Doesn't sound like my thing unless I get to play the simulated shooter."

"You sick bastard," Tom said, laughing.

Tom looked at the time, then placed his bag on top of the media cart he was going to take to his classroom. "Shit, I gotta get going. Gotta get that DVD player all set up before the herd arrives."

"What are you showing?" Saunders asked.

Tom Corona smiled, pulled a DVD out of his bag, and handed it to Saunders.

"*Dawn of the Dead*?" Saunders said.

"Using the *Monsters* book," Tom said. "You know how students love that zombie shit. The book's actually got some pretty good commentary if you really dig into it. What better way to keep them engaged than by giving them something they like? Besides, all the hiring committees are looking for someone who is interested in engaging students with more pop culture."

The previous year the department had banned the use of literature in all composition classes and had standardized the textbooks. "This is not creative writing," Crawford wrote in a memo, after a fellow adjunct had been caught using *The Great Gatsby* in class. The selection of "readers" to use with *Au Revoir* had been narrowed down to two choices: *Great American Essays*, which had all the standards from Emerson to James Baldwin, and the bizarrely-themed reader called *Monsters*, with essays written about zombie movies that had no doubt come with some kickbacks to the department.

Saunders had gone with *Great American Essays*, and hence the theme of his course: "The Myth of the American Dream," which was cliché, but still better than zombies.

"So, let me get this straight," Saunders said, "you can't teach

The Great Gatsby, but you can show them a seventies zombie movie?"

Tom Corona smiled at him.

"Face it, Berlin. Literature with a capital L is dead. Hiring committees want to see that you're engaging your students with things they care about."

Tom was right. Maybe for the past twelve years he had been going about his business all wrong. It had sickened him to see the titles his fellow adjuncts chose for some of the literature classes. Not only were his colleagues assigning books like *Harry Potter*, but one guy even assigned the novelization of *Star Wars*.

Tom didn't have any ethical dilemmas about what he was doing. Did Tom Corona toss and turn at night because he felt like a fraud? Would Tom Corona ever consider committing suicide because he lost faith in his job and his girlfriend left him? If he'd ever had a girlfriend.

Then, all of the sudden, he felt sorry for Tom. As far as he could tell, Tom lived a solitary life. There had been a night, long ago, when Saunders was still with Kathy, and they spotted Tom sitting at a faux Irish pub by their apartment called EJ Malloy's, drinking an iced tea and eating dinner alone. Saunders had rushed Kathy through the bar holding his head down as they passed right behind Tom and slipped out to the back patio.

"I feel bad," she said, when Saunders quickly shot down the suggestion they invite Tom to dine with them. It's true that she'd always been more empathetic than him.

Kathy Stone is a better person than I am.

To redeem himself partly from the guilt of sins long ago, Saunders held the door while Tom pushed the media cart out of the mailroom. But when the cart got jammed on the doorsill and the projector slid off the cart and smashed on the concrete floor, Saunders let go of the door and headed for class.

He remembered that girl from the other night who had called him a nerd at the bar, and realized how it hurt him, and then he wished he could be someone else. Was it possible to plagiarize a life? And what about all the great writers of literature—didn't some of them steal? Certainly, out there somewhere, at that very moment, some anal-retentive English teacher was submitting the whole Western canon through Copycat.

CHAPTER 12
PARTICIPATION POINTS

"The first rule of Book Club is that you don't talk about Book Club," announced George Glazer, as he opened the door for Saunders. Who could fault a guy wearing a t-shirt that said "Nietzsche Is Peachy" and had referred to the day's event as "Super Book Sunday"?

"The second rule," George said, before handing Saunders a cup, "is that you have to try my wife's sangria. We always do a regional drink to go with our reading."

The Glazers' home was a quaint little place just over the aqua-green Vincent Thomas Bridge in San Pedro. The second thing George did—after the sangria—was hand him a sticker to wear as a nametag.

Their living room walls were splattered with prints, including Picasso's rendition of Don Quixote, bought on a trip George and his wife Kelley had taken to Madrid last summer, which had been the impetus for selecting the novel.

George brought Saunders into the living room and introduced him to everybody. Saunders recognized a few faces and nodded.

The conversation was already heated by the time he'd arrived. The female attraction level was mostly disappointing, impaling any hope he had. But then he noticed an attractive blonde he'd never seen before, sipping sangria and flipping through the pages of her book.

"I found the novel to be extremely homoerotic," said a super-sized hunchback (really just a tall woman with ridiculously broad shoulders to accompany her bad posture) who Saunders had squeezed next to on the Glazers' wheat-colored couch.

"There's definitely something going on between Sancho and Don," said her pockmark-faced husband, sitting on the other side.

"And what's with all that donkey imagery?" said another guy by the name of Paul Cross, who apparently worked at the high school with Glazer's wife Kelley.

These were his people. The only people who still met and discussed books no matter how haphazardly or ridiculous those discussions were. And where had they come from? And how had he gotten himself into a fix like this? Did he really need to make new friends?

"Did you know Cervantes died on the same day as Shakespeare?" Glazer's mouth dropped open as if to dramatize the shock of it all. His tongue was dark red from the sangria. "I just find that incredibly fascinating."

If George had been his student, Saunders would've told him how "fascinating" was one of those words that didn't need to be modified by "incredibly."

Poor George. He was one of those guys whose life you'd fear for if he were ever thrown in the county jail; the kind of guy who joined wine clubs, planned group trips to museums, had a paper weight on his desk in the shape of the Eiffel Tower; the kind of guy who bought cheap tickets to the opera just to feel cultured, but always fell asleep; the kind of guy who once even spent a whole summer reading *Finnegans Wake* just to show everyone how smart he was.

"I suppose the real question we should be asking," said Bill Gandy, who Saunders once served on a "norming" committee with, back when he was still kissing ass and hoping for a full-time gig, "is what relevance does a novel like this have for us in the twenty-first century?"

The super-sized hunchback bunched her big legs up beneath her on the couch, and flipped through her book, which had post-it notes all over it; and for the next few seconds, Saunders watched as she kept licking her lips as if about to answer the question.

"I think in order for us to answer that question," she finally said, "we first have to ask who the 'us' is? I mean the world of Cervantes is a world in which every woman is either a princess or a prostitute."

"Sounds good to me," Paul Cross said, to the scowl of every woman in the living room, who seemed ready to throw their sangria at him.

"Leave it to Paul to piss everyone off in the first half hour," joked George.

"Nothing new," said Paul, smiling.

"Penny for your thoughts, Berlin?" George said.

On his way to the Glazers, Saunders had stopped at a Ralph's to buy cigarettes and a bottle of wine to contribute to the festivities, and gotten caught up in the Super Bowl rush hour line, with people stocking up on beer and pretzels and various bottles of booze.

Saunders spit an orange peel from the sangria back into his cup.

"Who's winning the game?" he said. Everybody laughed. George Glazer laughed a little too hard, as if he pitied him, maybe for knowing about his recent break up with Kathy. Still, the attention felt good. Maybe he could get used to it. Saunders began to relax.

"I don't know," Saunders said. "To me, Don Quixote is a hero. A universal symbol of the struggle for justice, the righting of wrongs. I really don't think it has much to do with donkeys."

Not bad. All that and he hadn't even completed the first hundred pages. He was proud of himself. Of course, this didn't mean he hadn't cheated a bit and read that somewhere on the Internet before coming over, but nobody needed to know.

"Hmm…," said the attractive blonde. "That's a very romantic opinion, I guess. One with which I would have to disagree. I think this novel is very satiric and actually pokes fun at the idea of universals."

"Exactly," the super-sized hunchback said, rolling her eyes. "Universals are *so* forty years ago. Doesn't that just take us down that same old slippery slope of the master narrative? I mean, who is to decide what is universal? White men?"

Why had he decided on coming anyway? Had he really expected to meet a pretty single woman worth talking to? He wondered if it didn't have more to do with a fear of staying home too long, as his mind would start thinking about too many things— like that damn suicide note he should've been writing.

"It *is* interesting," Kelley said. "Because if you read the criticism on the book, they seem to split into these two camps: those who interpret the novel as romantic idealism and those who interpret it as debunking the master narrative."

If she had been his student, Saunders would've slighted her for the use of a banned word like "interesting."

"But what does Cervantes want us to know? Is he being ironic?" asked George. "When Don Quixote builds his armor from the rusted scraps of his great–grandfather's armor, are we supposed to laugh or be in awe?"

"Both," said Kelley. "We're supposed to do both. That is the magic of this book."

"I just think he's crazy," Paul Cross said.

"I think his quest is literally crazy but metaphorically important," said George. "By trying to recast the armor that once protected his great-grandfathers, he's trying to fix what has spent many long years being 'stored and forgotten' in that corner."

"In other words," the attractive blonde said, "he's nostalgic for an era gone past; which is exactly what Cervantes is making fun of."

"Yeah, but there's a difference between nostalgia for the past, and trying to fix its wrongs," said Saunders.

Fatal error. The attractive blonde just looked at him and scoffed.

"I just love it when men explain things to me," she said.

The whole room went silent. He saw the super-sized hunchback squeeze her husband's hand. It was time to go.

"Whatever he is," said Bill Gandy, saving the day, "Paul's right. The dude is frickin' nuts."

On his drive back to Long Beach, Saunders wondered if he could find a place to pull off on the Vincent Thomas Bridge, and just get it over with. But given the vertigo he felt watching the documentary about the Golden Gate jumpers, he knew he could never go through with it. If only he weren't so afraid of heights. It just wouldn't do. There had to be a better way. A more noble ending.

CHAPTER 13
Coarse Desscription

The first unsettling moment of the semester came at the next class meeting.

"To argue well," Saunders said, "you need to do more than just assert your own position, you need to enter the conversation, by first deeply engaging in the viewpoints of others to serve as a launching pad."

The day's journal assignment was for students to write an argument for a position they supported, followed by another paragraph in which they wrote an argument against that same position. Then afterward, the class would play a guessing game as to where the student really stood on the issue.

The day had started off all right.

Corey Goodwin was the first to raise his hand and read his two paragraphs on the legalization of marijuana. And, of course, everyone guessed his stance correctly. He was followed by Hafiz Amad who wrote about the use of steroids in professional sports. Then Jonathan Tsuyuki addressed the issue of technology in the classroom in which he argued, not two different sides exactly, but only one, which was that it could be used by teachers to post video lectures that students could watch at home, allowing time to do something more in the classroom. This sounded like a nightmare to Saunders. Twice the work for the same pay? Jonathan got an "F" for the day. Greedy little bastard.

Next up was Vanessa Rivas.

"Some people argue," she said, "that a fat tax is unfair and discriminatory. After all, why should anyone have to pay for two airplane seats just because of their weight? Others argue that people should take responsibility for their weight and do more to control their problem, like exercising and not eating as much."

There was silence in the classroom when she finished.

"Well," Saunders said. "Is she in favor of the tax or is she against it?"

"Against," Kendall Johnson said.

"Against," Fabian Lopez said.

"Against," Erica Benavides said.

Saunders made a mental note not to call on Vanessa Rivas anymore. He looked around the room. That was all for the votes. Others were nodding their heads in agreement. Nobody wanted to believe that little Vanessa Rivas was actually in favor of charging fat people for an extra airline ticket; not even Saunders wanted to go there.

"I would agree with that," he said. "She's against it."

"No way!" Adam Rowan said. "She's definitely for it."

Vanessa nodded her head, and turned around to look at Adam who was sitting behind her.

"That guy's right," she said. "I'm all for it!"

Adam smiled and Saunders felt his face turn red. It had been wishful thinking on his part to think she was against such a motion. After all, not everyone wanted to avoid conflict like he did this semester.

"Adam guessed correctly," Saunders said. "Well done. Any particular thing that helped you decide?"

Adam thought about it for a minute, and then said, "She didn't use the first person. One of the telltale signs that someone is lying."

"You want to back that statement up with any evidence?" Saunders said.

"There have been studies," Adam said. "I read an article about it. If I can find it, I'll bring it in."

"Maybe there ought to be an ugly face tax?" Tess Mackenzie, a significantly larger white girl, who often came to class wearing her pajamas, said to Vanessa.

Vanessa Rivas looked surprised, but not intimidated by Tess's size.

"If that were the case, then you would be paying double," she said.

"Hey, hey, hey," Saunders said. "Everyone be nice to each other."

Adam shook his head as if to say, aren't you going to do anything more about this? But what could Saunders do? All he really wanted to do was excuse the class or, better yet, walk away and let them hash it out themselves. But it wasn't time yet. He had miles to go. He was still stopped in those snowy woods.

"Anyone else want to read their journal?" Saunders said it half-assed, hoping no one did. Then Beverly MacDowell, an African-American woman around 50, who had returned to school, raised her hand.

"As a mother of two teenage boys, I feel strongly about the need to do something about gun violence. Unfortunately, people are being killed with guns every day and it's only when students in a white school get shot that all of us start paying attention. But people where I come from know this is something that threatens us every day. On the other hand, some people argue that it's already too late. That there are just too many guns out there and that criminals will find a way to buy guns anyway."

"Great job, Beverly," Saunders said.

Adam raised his hand.

"Technically, gun violence has declined by 20% in the last decade."

"Tell that to the people in my neighborhood," Beverly interrupted.

"The only thing that stops a bad guy with a gun is a good guy with a gun," said Adam. "The reason the Second Amendment exists in the first place is to protect us from the tyranny of the government. You can bet it's only a matter of time before they come knocking at your door."

"There weren't any AR-15 assault rifles in 1776," Beverly said.

"I'm saying you never know what could happen," Adam said. "This government, and the people running it, will do anything to hold onto their power."

This notion that the government was somehow going to take all of Adam's guns away was as paranoid as the idea that a handful of people were secretly running the world. Saunders had always imagined some right-wing wackos in the sticks of Montana coming up with a conspiracy theory about guns, not some kid attending community college in Long Beach. The left had its conspiracies too, such as 9/11 being some kind of inside job orchestrated by the Bush regime to destabilize the Middle East.

"Wasn't it Thoreau who said even voting for what you think is right is doing nothing? That men are feebly expressing their desires. When what is needed is real action?" Adam looked at Saunders.

They would be reading Thoreau in a couple of weeks. Was it possible Adam had thrown out his name as a way of impressing Saunders? Or was this merely a coincidence?

"Thoreau, by the way," Adam said, "was in favor of guns. Grew up with them. Said it was one of the most important parts of his education."

Where had Adam come to know so much about Thoreau? Saunders wanted to ask, but didn't. He had loved Thoreau at a young age, even younger than Adam, just fresh out of high school, back when he, too, had believed in changing the world. But despite that, when he taught him every year, his interest in Thoreau's idealistic views of things faded along with the dissipation of his own views.

Beverly MacDowell rolled her eyes at Adam's comment about Thoreau.

"Besides that," Adam said, "California already has some of the strictest gun laws on the books. They're obviously not keeping anybody safer."

Saunders watched as Beverly shook her head and looked down at her desk. Though debate was healthy, he could see she wasn't feeling the need to defend herself to this white guy and Adam was clearly looking to engage in an argument over his pet cause.

"What about a nuclear weapon?" Saunders said. "Should we have a right to bear that? Or does two hundred and fifty years of technology make a difference? Does the Second Amendment grant that?"

Beverly smiled and looked back at Adam.

"If that's your argument," he said, "then might as well limit the First Amendment to quill and ink."

"Sticks and stones?" Saunders said.

"Touché," Adam said. "But, an assault rifle is not a WMD, and, are you saying words have never killed anybody?"

Despite his own staunch defense of the First Amendment, Saunders couldn't pretend that words had never been used to incite violence.

"It's not the same," Saunders said.

"No, it isn't," Beverly said. "Words have not killed anybody in and of themselves."

A talking point he often used himself, but which, in some ways, was a lie and contradicted everything he tried to teach his students each semester, that words were their own weapons of mass destruction. Or at least, at one time he'd believed them to be. He hated it when people blamed speech on violence; but the moment Beverly said this, she swung open the door for an increasingly frustrated and defensive retort by Adam, "Neither have guns."

Beverly shrugged her shoulders.

"Not to mention, the way they want to change the law may require a background check for inheritance. Which means my family would need a background check for my father's guns. Nobody in the government has a right to tell me what I can and can't inherit."

As if orchestrated, Adam's cell phone went off.

"That your father calling?" Saunders said to Adam. The class laughed.

Embarrassed, Adam had taken his phone out of his pocket and switched it off.

"Nah," he said, "I don't have a father."

It was time to change the subject.

CHAPTER 14
Handouts

Adam showed up to the next class wearing an army-green t-shirt with a red rifle across the front of it that said, "Protect Your Rights." Saunders's left eye began to twitch again.

For homework that day, he assigned a reading of the first fifteen paragraphs of Emerson's "Self-Reliance."

"Is it enough," Saunders said, "to 'trust thyself'?"

This had been the question he posed for the day's journal.

Only Adam had raised his hand.

"When the earliest settlers came to the New World, they came in search of a fresh start. They came for new opportunities and new freedoms that hadn't even been dreamed up yet, but would eventually be drafted in one of the most revolutionary texts of all time, our Constitution. Emerson's notion of 'trusting thyself' is one that I ascribe to greatly. With enough hard work and determination, you can be anything you want. If you are born into a working-class family in Mexico, for instance, you might not have the opportunity to move up to being middle class or even wealthy. That's why so many of them want to come here. To me, this is what makes America great. The idea of individual opportunity. The ability to climb the ladder. Unlike a Communist country, we have the freedom to be ourselves. You can be whatever you want to be. It's an equal playing field. So Emerson's right: the more you trust yourself, the greater chance you will be able to achieve that dream. But to sum it up, to trust thyself is about all you can do because you can't trust the government. We must fight to preserve that dream as more and more constraints are being put on us as citizens of a government that is too involved in our lives, and the individual is less able to make choices for himself."

This was the first time Saunders had heard "communism" used negatively in a while. Although he never called himself one, becoming a Marxist (in theory only) was practically required of anyone in the English Department.

In some ways, he could understand some of the paranoia conservative talk show hosts had about liberal professors. Most of the papers he wrote during his college years were Marxist interpretations of literary works firstly, to ensure he got an "A", and secondly, because it was the easiest interpretation of a literary text you could make. Much easier than having to dig into all those symbols and metaphors.

Adam began to drift off and turn his journal into a rant against taxes, immigration, "government handouts." Saunders had to resist interrupting him. If only an orchestra would appear and start playing music like on the Academy Awards.

"For a moment there, I was worried we were going to agree," Saunders said, finally cutting Adam off mid-sentence.

Adam smiled.

"Yeah," he said. "I would've had to really question myself if I agreed with one of my professors."

"That's very Emersonian of you."

Saunders turned to the class.

"But what might be the problem with only 'trusting thyself'? Is it really enough? Or are there constraints that we cannot escape in society?"

Nobody said anything. The room got so still he thought the motion-sensor lights would go off. They either didn't know the answer or hadn't read the text. All the students stared straight down at their paper. Except Adam, who finally couldn't take it and raised his hand.

"I'd say it's just the opposite. People don't trust themselves enough and end up trusting unaccountable institutions, like the federal government. Isn't this our history? Fear and lack of trust, the motive behind all our actions? What is fear, but a consequence of not being self-reliant?"

Adam had a point.

Wasn't this also Saunders's own problem? Hadn't his life been ruled by fear? He had never been able to trust himself. He never trusted himself to fully become a writer. Never trusted himself to go after a full-time position. Never trusted himself to try to stop Kathy from walking out that door. Now he couldn't even trust himself to finish the job of committing suicide.

"You can have all the courage you want," Saunders finally said, "but that's not going to change the institutional racism and sexism in society. I may be brave enough to trust myself, but that might not be enough."

"Your fingers are smoother than mine," Kathy once told him, while he gave her a massage. She hadn't meant anything by it, but she still managed to get a rise out of him, which led to a fight when he accused her of trying to emasculate him.

"How disappointing," she told him later, her eyes closed like they often were as she searched for the right words. "That you'd be so conditioned by a gender construct to get mad at me."

By the end of their relationship, had there been any trust? His trust in himself, her trust in him? For too long, he had been trapped in a theme. For too long he believed in life, liberty, and the pursuit of happiness. But the dream died. He needed a way out. He knew the way, of course, but when? And how long would he hold on?

After class, Adam hung around while the next group of students started to trickle in and Saunders had to ask them to leave so he could lock up the door until their professor came.

He erased the board while Adam stood there with his green rifle shirt and camouflaged backpack.

"What can I do for you, Adam?" he said.

"I just wanted to tell you that I won't be here next time," he said.

"Ok," Saunders said, reciting a well-rehearsed line. "Just keep up with the reading."

"What about the paper?" Adam said.

Saunders had forgotten all about the first paper. A personal narrative about a significant change.

"The personal narrative, really?" he could hear some of his colleagues saying. "They're eighteen. What experience could they possibly have to write about? Plus, how can you even evaluate it?"

"I guess it'll be late," Saunders said, as he grabbed his bag and began walking to the door, Adam behind him.

"Can I email it to you beforehand?"

"That's fine. Just email it when you can," Saunders said. "And we'll go from there."

"Interesting class, by the way," Adam said. "I'm really enjoying it."

"Thanks," Saunders said. "You sure like to argue, don't you?"

"It'd be un-American of me not to," Adam said, pulling on his shirt to draw attention to it.

"Well, you know, I probably agree with you about a lot more than you think I do," Saunders said. "You're right about the American Dream. This country doesn't have the opportunities it used to. It seems hard for anyone to get ahead these days. I'm not sure we agree on the reasons for it, but it's true, maybe, we shouldn't always depend on the government."

Adam laughed and set his backpack on top of an empty desk, just as Saunders was ready to get out of there.

"I guess I'm just looking for a sense of purpose," Adam said.

"Aren't we all?" Saunders said. "Well, stay in school. That's a good place to find one." He didn't even believe the words as he said them. He just knew they were the words a teacher was supposed to tell his student. What he really wanted to tell him was that trying to change the world was a futile attempt.

"That's what teachers back home always tried to tell me," said Adam. "I never thought I'd be back in school."

"Where's home?"

"Michigan."

"What brought you out here?"

"The service," said Adam. "But I stayed for a girl. I stayed and she left."

"Ain't that the way it goes. How long were you in the service?"

"Almost six years," Adam said. "Medical discharge or I'd probably still be over there. It's kinda weird being in school with some of these kids. We look the same. We're about the same age. But we're not the same."

Saunders could have never imagined joining the military at eighteen. Had this just been a sign of his own privilege? Yes. He had never had to make that choice, had he? Even when he registered for the draft at eighteen, he had written "Conscientious Objector" on the bottom of the card just in case there were ever another one. His privileged idea of being politically engaged was working for the Democratic Party during the election of Bill Clinton in 1992. It was the first presidential election he was going to be able to vote in and he and his first girlfriend had signed up to work for the Democratic party and a couple times even set up tables outside of an old clothing store called Mervyn's and tried to get people interested in democracy. In a box somewhere, he still had a certificate thanking him for electing Bill Clinton as the 42nd president of the United States.

"By the way," Saunders said. "Didn't mean to put you on the spot the other day about your father."

"It was nothing," Adam said.

"I won't pry, but I know how you feel. I don't have a father either," Saunders said.

"It's pretty common," Adam said. "Was yours a suicidal alcoholic, too?"

"No. He died in a fire."

This was the first time he'd used this lie to explain away his father. He even surprised himself.

When they got to the door, Saunders froze. In the corner of his eye, he caught a familiar silhouette walking down the hallway. Kathy was heading straight his way—as if all this thinking about her, had conjured her up in the real world. He wanted to look, having not seen her in almost two months, but instead he leaped back inside the classroom, dragging Adam with him. Saunders put two fingers to his own pulse to feel how fast his heart was beating.

"What was that?" Adam said. "Are you all right?"

Saunders closed his eyes, annoyed that Adam was still there to witness this. He sat down at a desk by the door, until he could presume Kathy had already walked by.

"Sorry," he told Adam. "It's nothing. Just give me a sec." He pulled out some bottled water from his bag and took a sip of it.

Adam peeked outside the window of the classroom door to see what was happening. Saunders screwed the lid back on his bottle of water and stuffed it back into his bag, waited a moment, then stood up.

"The coast is clear," Adam said. "She's gone."

Saunders looked at him, then quickly realizing it had been that obvious, caught himself cind feigned an unconvincing apathy, which he couldn't hold for very long.

"Can you keep a secret?"

"Of course," Adam said.

"We have history."

He told him about Crawford and Kathy, which was probably more information about his life than he'd ever given a student and wasn't sure why he had chosen to tell Adam.

"That's messed up," Adam said, "And if you were my friend and not my teacher, I'd probably have used a different verb."

"At least you know what a verb is," Saunders said. He shut the lights off in the classroom as they made their way out the door. Just then the professor who occupied the classroom after him approached, a short frail-looking woman with bags under her eyes and a Starbuck's coffee cup in her hand that had "Carol" written at the top of it.

"What time does your class end?" she said.

He thought about it, then told her.

"That's what I thought," she said, sighing, and looking at her phone. "Some days you're still here and some days you're not. I wish you would be more consistent so I could know."

She refused to let him continue holding the door for her, then stormed inside the classroom, her class behind her, which made him feel guilty like he had done something wrong. Adam pulled out his phone and showed Saunders there was still technically two minutes left of class time.

"You know what Emerson says," Adam told him. "A foolish consistency is the hobgoblin of little minds."

CHAPTER 15
Role Call

That weekend, Saunders decided to get out of his apartment and meet up with some old college buddies. Maybe he could talk to them instead of vomiting up everything about his life to a student he had just met. He had known Mike Livingston and Kevin Neely from grad school, two fiction writers at one time who both had gotten jobs as tenure-track faculty at two local community colleges. Though he considered them friends, he had seen them less frequently over the years, both married with a kid, a wife, a house.

"And this is the walkway," Mike said, showing him a picture on his phone of the walkway he'd just laid down in his backyard. "And this is where we'll put the new patio furniture."

Mike was the kind of guy who wore shorts with tennis shoes and white socks even during winter. The kind of guy who wanted nothing more than to own a house with a BBQ and a fridge full of craft beer.

"Fantastic," Kevin said. He also had pictures of his house on his phone.

It was Saunders's idea to meet at The Reno Room, a dark bar near his place that served up Mexican food from the restaurant next door. The bar still had an old neon sign hanging in front of it, and on the walls were pictures of semi-naked women, and every time he stared at them he expected them to grow old like on the Haunted Mansion ride at Disneyland.

In the twenty minutes they'd been there, neither of his friends had mentioned a book. Saunders thought back to their college days, remembering how all three of them insisted they would never stop writing and would never teach composition. And yet now they were. He couldn't figure out who wanted to kill themselves more.

"Buying a place is a great investment," Mike said. "My equity just keeps going up. Berlin, you should really get in on this shit."

"And teach eight classes a semester?" he said.

Over the five years with Kathy, there had been occasional talk on her side about buying a house.

"It's what grown-ups do," she told him once.

"When they can afford it," he had replied.

Eventually, he figured, the disparity between their salaries would have become an issue in their relationship, despite their doing the exact same work. After all, no matter how much of a feminist Kathy was, no woman really respected a man who made less than she did.

"I'm still going through puberty, guys," he said. "I'll catch up."

"Dude," Kevin said, "get out those full-time applications before it's too late."

"Too late?"

"They'll stigmatize you."

"For being an adjunct?" Saunders said.

Mike looked at Kevin.

"Truth be told," Mike said. "Adjuncts aren't known to be very good teachers."

Kevin laughed in agreement.

"I'd be surprised if you get any interviews, anyway," Mike said. "Too bad you're not Latino. That's who they're looking for right now."

Saunders stabbed his gums with a tortilla chip from a basket the bartender had placed in front of him.

He hadn't eaten all day. In fact, he hadn't been eating much at all lately. He had lost at least ten pounds since his breakup with Kathy. Smoking a pack a day certainly helped. He couldn't complain about it really. On the outside, he looked healthier than he had for years. Of course, he didn't bother telling his friends he'd started smoking again as they'd only lecture him.

The subject soon changed from their houses to their students.

"Honestly," Mike said, "if I have to read one more paper about the legalization of pot. Is it me or have you guys noticed that this year's students are the worst since we've started teaching?"

"They always seem bad to me," Kevin said. "They can't read. They can't spell. They can't think. All they care about is playing with their phones."

A young couple, probably in their early twenties, sat down next to them. The girl was stunning and reminded him of a young Hope Sandoval from Mazzy Star. The guy was not so stunning, unshaven with only patches of facial hair, trying his best to look hip, which he was young enough to succeed at.

"I thought you were gonna rob me when you slipped me that note," the girl said to the guy. They seemed to have just met.

"No," the guy said. "I just thought you were cute. How long

have you worked at the bank?"

"I've been a teller for about a year," she said.

And when the guy ordered shots and the girl didn't refuse, Saunders knew she liked him.

"If I have to read one more essay that begins with 'In today's society,'" Kevin said.

"Or how about this one?" Mike said. "This one's hilarious. I had a student write in a paper that baby Jesus was born to Mother Theresa."

They both burst out in laughter. Saunders couldn't tell them apart anymore. Were they just manifestations of the same person?

"The other day, a student wrote, 'skip row,' instead of 'skid row,'" Mike said. "I thought that was a good one."

Kevin laughed again.

"And is it too much to ask that they staple their own papers? Every semester I have to tell them this isn't high school. I don't carry around a stapler with me."

Saunders watched as the girl put her head into the guy's chest. The guy put his arm around her. They sat by an open door and outside Saunders saw the flickering red lights of an ambulance pass by.

"Who were you at eighteen?" he said to his friends.

He knew who he was. A "C" student sitting on the lawn of a community college smoking cigarettes.

"I had a stapler," Mike said. "That's for sure."

Maybe that's why they could afford houses and he couldn't. He saw them look at one another.

"Did I tell you I finished the bathroom?" Mike said, exclusively to Kevin, pulling up more pictures on his phone.

To be great is to be misunderstood.

Emerson was wrong about that. To be great is to be *understood.* Galileo was understood, they just didn't like what he had to say.

Saunders saw a long tattooed white arm cross the path of his vision with a hot plate of food. The burrito he had ordered finally arrived.

"Careful, hot plate," the waitress said.

At least now, he had something to do.

CHAPTER 16
WAC

From: hcrawford@lbcc.edu

To: English-Faculty@lbcc.edu

Subject: Housekeeping & WAC Job

Good Morning Friends,

Happy Friday to you!

By now with the early weeks of the semester coming to an end, you should finally be feeling a bit more relaxed—-at least until that first batch of papers arrives!

A couple housekeeping items:

Please remember to leave your classroom in a timely manner after each class. I've had a couple complaints already that some of the faculty are not doing that when there's another class waiting.
Also, it's your job to clean out the refrigerator in the breakroom not the office staff's. Joanne found lunch bags from last semester still in there.

Now on to bigger news:

I'm happy to officially announce I've been given authorization by President S. King to create a new Writing across the Curriculum (WAC) job in the English Department. This will be a tenure-track position so adjuncts please consider applying!

Why create this position now? Let me just clarify.

1. WAC is a pedagogy developed over the past thirty years that contains approaches to instruction and writing that we must implement in order to have a credible WAC program.

2. The new WAC job should be awarded to a person with a background in or at least be willing to get training in WAC.

3. Even though some of you have objected to creating this new position, both the Writing Task Force (WTF) and the director of GWAR (Graduate Writing Assessment Requirement) have recommended it. So I say let's do this:

A new WAC coordinator will help us implement a WAC approach and develop a successful WAC program!

-Harry

CHAPTER 17
COARSE REQUIREMENTS

"Broke out of Chester gaol, last night, one James Rockett, a very short well set fellow, pretends to be a schoolmaster, of a fair complexion, and smooth fac'd. Had on when he went away, a light colored camblet coat, a blue cloth jacket, without sleeves, a check shirt, a pair of old dy'd leather breaches, gray worsted stockings, a pair of half worn pumps, and an almost new beaver hat; his hair is cut off, and wears a cap; he is a great taker of snuff, and very apt to get drunk; he has with him two certificates, one from some inhabitants in Burlington county, Jersey, which he will no doubt produce a pass. Who ever takes up and secures said Rockett in any gaol, shall have two Pistols reward, paid by October 27, 1756" –
SAMUEL SMITH, Gaoler

-advertisement for a "runaway schoolmaster"
Pennsylvania Gazette, November 25, 1756

Saunders had seen this advertisement in a textbook called *Rereading America* that he used one semester when he taught critical thinking. In the same book, he also read a list of duties of the earliest American teachers, mostly indentured servants whose price of passage to the New World were to teach their master's children. But for the Puritans, being a teacher carried with it other duties too, spiritual duties, like leading the choir on Sundays or ringing the bell for public worship. But the one Saunders loved best of all was number five on the list of duties: digging graves.

Sometimes, he already felt like this was part of his job description. Maybe it wasn't a coincidence that *graves* and *grades* were only one letter apart. Every morning when he left for work, he grabbed his blazer, his briefcase, and his shovel. He certainly had enough experience digging holes, which reminded him of when he worked for his Uncle David for two years out of high school.

Uncle David ran a construction business to stop houses from subsiding and stabilize the foundation. Part of the job involved digging holes, which was about the only thing Saunders was good at. Once it got past that point and actually involved some skill and coordination, the other guys would take over. But he was good at digging holes and dug them for two full years. Long days of labor, he came home sunburned and drenched in sweat. He hated it. Later, Uncle David admitted he only hired Saunders to convince him of the necessity of going to college.

"You want to dig holes for the rest of your life?"

Little did he know.

Saunders thought about that old adage, "Those who can't do, teach." But what about those who can't do or teach? Dig graves? Ring the church bells? Lead the church choir? No. They become the chair of the department. Or maybe just sleep with the chair of the department? At least Kathy had understood the humor of the acronyms used in the email threads.

"Don't they realize Gwar's a band that dresses up in freaky *Road Warrior* meets *Predator* monster costumes and throws fake blood on their audience?" she had said once.

To think, there was a time when they could laugh together. Would Crawford have understood that joke? It didn't matter now. For all Saunders knew, he had already lost her by then. He just didn't know it yet. Or had she lost him? Or had they both lost themselves? Or maybe an occasional laugh was all they'd ever had? And who was the joke on now?

He was an indentured servant all right. But not even tenure allowed passage to a New World. Like an indentured servant, nobody dragged him into it. He had chosen his path.

Sometime at the end of the week, Adam Rowan emailed him his paper.

The subject matter was "Missed Class."

Dear Sir,

I just wanted to thank you again for letting me turn in essay #1 early. Hope this is okay. Also, thanks again for the inspiring class the other day. It was good chatting!

Your student,

Adam

Though he was embarrassed now by their conversation, Saunders smirked at Adam's finding him inspiring and calling him "sir." He hit the reply button and wrote the same generic response he had already told him in the classroom. *No problem, Adam. Just keep up with the reading.*

Almost immediately, a reply came back.

BTW, hypothetical question: What if you could do something that would potentially change the world but the risks would be enormous? Would you do it?

Saunders wrote back.

I guess it depended what it was and what kind of change we're talking about.

Adam replied:

A good change. Let's say. A just change. Say it was your boss, for instance—that Crawford guy you told me about. Say you knew something about him that could get him to step down. Something you had thought about for a long time. Would you feel obligated to do something?

Saunders replied:

My gut instinct is to say yes. But, of course, it depends on what you're talking about. You're not talking about anything illegal, are you? What are you talking about anyway?

Adam replied, failing to address the second part of his email:

Thanks for the advice Professor!

No problem, Saunders wrote back, wondering what Adam was on about. He'd never known how to sign his name in student emails so sometimes he didn't sign his name at all. Professor seemed too formal and Berlin too informal. Occasionally, he'd signed it Prof. Saunders or Prof. S. But this time, he just used his initials, *B.S.,* then clicked open the attachment.

CHAPTER 18

ASSIGNMENTS

"What if something was stolen from your country?" asked one of our Iraqi interpreters, Hakim, who was probably one of the nicest guys I had ever known. "What if someone stole your Liberty Bell and held it for ransom?"

Actually, Hakim was really a Kurd and as a young kid, had seen his father get tortured, and later on had even gone to a University somewhere in Tennessee. He worked as an interpreter for the Iraqi Security Forces where I was stationed in Mosul, and he often went on missions with us.

The truth is I was embarrassed to let on that I didn't even know what he was talking about, that I didn't even know what the Liberty Bell was.

"I must've skipped that chapter in high school," I said. For all I knew it could've been the Taco Bell sign. And if somebody had stolen Taco Bell, I probably would've noticed it more. Here I was, a twenty-year old punk kid with teenage acne, in the middle of a warzone, and I needed an Iraqi Kurd to explain to me about a symbol of liberty in my own country because I didn't know shit.

"We'd cut their huevos off," said Sgt. Glassic, who was in the same platoon as me.

They were discussing the looting of the museum of Baghdad just after the war had gotten started, which had been a devastating event for the many Iraqis who felt as if the essence of who they were had been taken.

Thats when the mortars started falling.

Sgt. Harrison busted in and told us, "Grab your shit! We're moving out."

By the time we got a couple Humvees through the main gate of the barracks, we were taking fire.

I don't want to fucking die, I kept telling myself. Not now. As we headed up the road we passed a bridge and I could hear bullets richocheting off the armor of our vehicle, as we headed toward another part of the city where two other Humvees needed backup. Richochet wasn't the right word anyway, it was hailing bullets everywhere. Besides richochet was just some fancy French word, and we were a long way off from Paris.

I noticed somebody had run over a dog trying to cross the street. It lay there twitching, its ears turned into bloody sponges. Sgt. Duncan had said not to stop for anything, not even a child. Our attackers liked to put women, children, dogs, whatever they could in the road as a diversion.

Suddenly Sgt. Glassic screamed, "We're being ambushed!"

I saw two guys hunched down at the side of one of the buildings. Before I had a chance to aim at them, one of the guys jumped out and pointed his gun right at me. I heard bullets hit the armor all around me, like tiny little bells ringing. I ducked down, then turned my gun around and shot at him. People were firing everywhere. We were moving fast, and I could hear more bullets ding the Humvee.

I'm only twenty, I said to God. Don't let me fucking die before I can legally drink. Not in Iraq. Not even in Paris. I wondered if God heard my plea, and then decided that He probably fucking didn't with all the gunfire and explosions all around. I wasn't even sure if He existed in the first place, but figured it probably wasn't the best time to be questioning it. That's when I heard the first blast…

His colleagues had been wrong about the flaws of the personal narrative, Saunders thought… in one respect—Adam Rowan definitely had something to write about. But in another respect, they'd also been right—how could Saunders evaluate Adam Rowan's real-life experience?

And yet, Adam had held up his end of the bargain by writing the essay, hadn't he? Now Saunders had to hold up his, by pinging red marks all over it.

A few semesters ago, the use of red ink to correct student papers had been prohibited in the department out of concern that it'd be perceived as too negative and stressful. A new study came out exploring human reactions to red as too emotionally charged. It had been suggested the faculty use softer purple pens to grade, but when Kathy moved out she had not only taken his heart, but all his purple pens.

After a while, Saunders stopped putting marks altogether on Adam's paper and just read. The truth is, it was good. Really good. What made it so good wasn't as much the writing itself, as the depiction of a lived experience. One reason Saunders had given up his own efforts to write is that he had nothing worth writing about. Sure, Hemingway said, "Write what you know," but that's easy when you're Hemingway. And Saunders definitely wasn't. Yet, here was his student, living like a real-life Hemingway character.

Brakes! screamed Sgt. Glassic. He steered our vehicle closer to the blast, still keeping his distance from it. Smoke and debris from the blast were rising high into the air. We braced for more blasts. Two soldiers staggered out of the vehicle, one covered in blood. The right door was ripped off, and I saw the gunner face down on the side of the road. Glassic sprinted over to the Humvee and returned a minute later, and got on the radio.

"We got casualties!" he screamed into the radio when he returned. Two seconds later that would have been me, I thought.

I also knew Hakim was in that Humvee and I was just starting to realize what that meant when the second blast hit.

Later, in the hospital, Sgt. Glassic came to visit me.

"Ever been to Philadelphia?" he asked.

"No, why?" I said.

"That's where they got the Liberty Bell," he said.

Philadelphia, I thought. If I ever get out of here, I'm going straight there and gonna wrap my arms around that Liberty Bell and thank God for letting me live.

I told Sgt. Glassic my plans.

"Just do me one favor," he said. "When you get there, find someone to fix the crack."

CHAPTER 19
Practice Test

Up until Saunders heard the helicopters, he had forgotten all about the active shooter drill on campus. The sirens and mock gunfire made it nearly impossible to keep lecturing, and he'd decided to end his class early. Members of the SWAT team in helmets, with large guns at their sides, positioned themselves behind bushes, ready to move into the Science building, next door to Humanities, to conduct the first of many simulated training exercises. Later, they would move into the Humanities building itself, where rumor had it they were going to stage a drill on the stairs.

Media vans pulled in from all the major news channels to cover the story. The south parking lot was blocked off and there were police cars and a large truck that said LBPD on it. Rabbits were running everywhere to find cover. Crowds of both faculty and students surrounded the building, watching the demonstration, but were kept behind police lines so only the volunteers participating could be inside the building.

Saunders wondered where Tom Corona was. With all the attention on the drill and the controlled chaos ensuing, he wondered if he should cancel his next class. Certainly, it'd be a good excuse. Maybe he'd just meet with them, and if the noise continued let them go home. Did people outside of the college, in the community at large, know what was happening? He heard more mock gunfire, put on his sunglasses, then moved up on a grassy hill so he could see better. That's when he ran into Ray Zapata. Without saying anything to Saunders, Ray lit his tobacco pipe, and sucked in the smoke.

"I was going to volunteer," he finally said. "But they already had enough hostages."

They laughed. Ray looked less like a college professor than he did a construction worker, wearing a torn dark blue flannel, jeans with a large chain full of keys hanging from his belt loop, and beige hiking boots. He had plumped up over the last few years, and Saunders had watched his uncut, messy hair turn white.

"I tried to tell them I've had thirty years' experience being a hostage," he said.

A group of firemen walked past the crowd and into the building. In the distance, Saunders heard more sirens and saw the paramedics arriving. A small group of simulated EMTs brought out a couple of giggling students on stretchers, waving at the crowd. One moaned, pretending to be injured, as they carried off his stretcher. Saunders even noticed a simulated bullet wound, with fake blood smeared on the student's lower abdomen. At the other side of the building, members of the SWAT team ran up the stairs to the second floor, their helmets bouncing on their heads with each step. Then more mock gunfire. Ray buried his lighter into the hole of his pipe and took another hit, then blew out the smoke.

"Drill, my ass," he said. "If this thing were real, these guys would be shitting their *pantalones*."

Saunders heard shouts from inside the building, men from

police units and SWAT units giving orders. Some of the crowd laughed. A few students and faculty *oohed* and *aahed* whenever a gun went off, or there was an explosion of some sort, or a member of the SWAT team appeared on the stairs. Everybody else remained quiet considering the show put on in front of them. It was like watching a live action show at Universal Studios. Two students with tennis rackets walked by, completely uninterested in what was happening…ignoring the sounds of mock gunfire as they made their way down campus toward the courts on the south side. Had everybody been expecting this? He waited to see the reaction of somebody who didn't know what was happening.

"Don't count on it," Zapata said. "This is Long Beach. Nothing fazes anybody. The other night I could've sworn I heard a gunshot in my neighborhood. In fact, I was positive. Even the wife woke up, asked me if that was a gunshot, then rolled over and started snoring."

"We're watching," Saunders said.

"That's just because we have to," Zapata said.

"Why's that?"

"It gives us the perfect excuse not to do anything," he said.

Paramedics brought more "wounded" but giggling students out of the building. Saunders overheard somebody say that inside they were drilling for an actual hostage crisis. Somebody else said that in a few minutes they were going to have a news conference and the Mayor of Long Beach was going to speak.

"Who the hell is the Mayor of Long Beach anyway?" Zapata asked.

"Wouldn't know him if he was standing right next to us," said Saunders.

Turns out he was.

Camera crews were out in full force now and Saunders could see them preparing a platform for the news conference as a woman powdered the mayor's face and a man smoothed out his suit. Next to them were two aides, both talking on their phones. Meanwhile the simulated shooting drill continued, but the action was dwindling in the Science building and the audience had begun to grow bored, some of the students returning to sending text messages or trickling off to their classes.

"Hello, members of this campus," said the mayor, to a shriek of feedback. "I stand with you today in my commitment to be prepared for the worst, and to be ready to keep our students, our faculty, and our community safe from harm."

"Shit," Zapata said. "Now that I can get shot in the classroom, I might as well have gone to Vietnam. And to think that's the only reason I went to college and became a teacher."

He started laughing.

"Ah well," he continued. "They probably weren't gonna take me anyway. Motherfucking draft board tried to tell me I was crazy one time. Can you believe that? Me crazy? I told them: 'You people are the ones who are crazy, not me.' Maybe I ought to just retire from it all anyway. The black train's coming you know."

Nobody was interested in what the mayor had to say. Some mock training exercises were still taking place in the building, but most of the crowds had gotten bored and left. Visually, it wasn't all that entertaining. Even the media got bored and seemed eager to fly off to the next drama.

"Hey, I wanna show you something," Ray said, tapping him on the shoulder. "You gotta see this thing I made. It's great. Come on up to the office and we'll have a smoke or something."

Once they were in Zapata's office, Saunders sat down across from his desk and Zapata asked him to grab a 2x4 at the side of his chair and hand it to him. When he did, Zapata got up, and placed it at the bottom of the door, then whipped out his pipe and lit it. Saunders lit a cigarette.

"Smoking ban my ass," Zapata said. Many of the younger new-hires were afraid of Ray and never confronted him, despite that everyone knew he still smoked in there. But Saunders felt para-noid that any minute somebody was going to knock on Zapata's office door and catch him in the act.

"Check this out," Zapata said, before sticking his pipe in his mouth while he reached under the desk and grabbed what looked like a glass box with mirrors on each side of it.

"Hit the light switch, will ya?" he asked.

But when it still wasn't dark enough, Zapata made sure each of the blinds covering the large window in his office were turned flat. He pulled out his lighter and lit a candle that had been placed in the middle of the case.

"I call this my hell box," Zapata said. "Isn't it great? Some-times, when shit's bad, I'll just stay in here all day and stare at it."

Saunders scooted his chair up and looked in the case, and could see the candle multiplied by all the mirrors.

"Maybe the draft board was right," he said. "Maybe you are crazy."

Ray laughed.

"Around here," Ray said, "I'm the only sane one, amigo." He took another puff off his pipe then looked into the box.

"Isn't it wonderful?" he said.

Ray was crazy all right, but there was nobody like him. Saunders had looked Ray up on Ratemyprofessors.com a few times in the past, and it turned out most of Ray's students appreciated him too, except for the occasional sourpuss who complained Ray told too many stories in class and didn't teach them anything.

Saunders stared at the torn envelope from a letter on Ray's desk, noticing the half-torn Liberty Bell stamp.

"That stamp reminds me of a student I have this semester," Saunders said. "Wrote an excellent paper about being a gunner in Iraq. If I didn't know the guy, I'd almost think he'd plagiarized it."

"I always tell them," said Zapata, "if you're gonna steal it, you're gonna have to make it better."

Saunders had about two minutes to rush to his next class. He said goodbye, sliding the 2X4 out of the way with his foot so he could open the door. The whole fourth floor of the Humanities building reeked of smoke. Saunders waited for the elevator just as he heard gunfire on the staircase one floor beneath him. The drill had moved into the Humanities building. He took the elevator to the first floor where his second class of the day was, and made his way down the hall toward his classroom just in time to see two EMTs come rushing around the corner, carrying a stretcher with

Tom Corona on it, smiling and waving at him, fake blood soaking through his shirt.

CHAPTER 20

Errant Nights

That Thursday night Saunders spent at 3636 reading *Don Quixote*. There was hardly anyone in the bar, except him and a couple playing pool. He enjoyed the bar best when nobody was putting money in the jukebox for songs that made him cringe, and there weren't other lonely men trying to talk to him.

He still had a long way to go before he finished the book, but he'd get there. If time allowed. He wanted to finish the novel before he killed himself, but as each day went by, and he became more certain he wanted to leave this world, he cared less about it. What would it matter if he finished *Don Quixote* before he died? Not like he could take its memory to the void. *Did I choose this book to keep me alive?* It was, after all, over 900 pages. But no, he had simply chosen it because George Glazer invited him to the book club. Which is to say, he hadn't really chosen it at all.

Then I have been deceived all along, responded Don Quixote.

"I ain't gonna lie to you," Phil said, "the saddest part in that book is the ending." He put two shot glasses in front of them, squatted down, and pulled a cold bottle of Jäger out of the freezer below the bar. Saunders watched as the thick black liquid filled the empty shot glass.

"Salud," he said, then took the shot.

"I know you're not there yet," Phil said. "So I don't want to give any spoilers."

Immediately, Phil poured them another shot. There had been some nights in the bar when Saunders had been so drunk and Phil so insistent that he ended up pouring out his drink onto the worn gray carpet beneath the bar just before he stumbled home. But those days were long ago. He never poured his drinks out anymore.

"It's just that in the end…" Phil said.

Saunders held up his finger to his mouth.

"I don't want to know," he said.

Phil handed him the second shot.

Saunders hadn't been there long, but was already beginning to feel the buzz from the two shots he'd just consumed.

It seems to me, señor, that all these misfortunes we've had recently are surely a punishment for the sin your grace committed against your order of chivalry…

His luck of having an empty bar wore out as the night went on and people from all the other bars began trickling in. 3636 had always been the last stop for everyone. Maybe that's something he liked about the place. The last stop before what? Before they passed out, threw up, or fucked each other? The last stop before they went to jail for drunk driving or dropped the keys and fell to their deaths from the apartment stairs? When the bar got crowded, he didn't want to be there. It depressed him more and after he settled his tab, which was far less than he'd drank (another reason he liked the place), he began the short walk home.

He made it up to the top of the stairs successfully and shooed away a possum there. His next-door neighbors kept food on their porch to feed two stray cats and it always attracted possums, skunks, and raccoons. One of the stray cats looked like David Bowie, one pupil larger than the other. Its front leg was all bandaged up. In truth, Saunders never paid much attention to them, but Kathy had always stopped to pet them. Maybe cats were in her future. Or maybe in his.

When he got inside, he made the bad decision of pouring himself some Seagram's from an old bottle with a sticky, tight lid. Since his refrigerator was empty, he had no mixers and all but a few freezer-dried ice cubes to put in it. It tasted awful and would contribute to the hangover he'd have after a short, restless sleep. But at the time, he wasn't thinking that far ahead.

He looked around his castle. What a shithole. The door knob to his bathroom lay on the floor in the hallway. Dishes were piled up in the sink. The couch, which he'd salvaged from the street one day, had an old Norton anthology replacing a missing leg.

No walkway. No patio. No BBQ. No pictures to proudly show on his phone.

With nothing to do, he logged onto Facebook. He saw he had another message in his inbox from Will.

Hey King, what's up with the Golden Gate bridge picture? Random! Anyway, I don't know if you got my last message so I thought I'd try again. I know you're not a beach guy, but I'm sitting here at the beach in the South of France and let me just tell you, I think you'd love the view from where I'm sitting. You can use your imagination for the rest. Anyway, leaving for the airport in a couple hours and will be in town for a couple days to do the night-time talk show circuit and shoot a video. Hit me up, loser!

It should have depressed him more to get this message, but he was distracted by a friend request from one Henry David Thoreau. Saunders clicked on the link and saw that whoever made the profile had certainly done his research: "I was an American author, naturalist, transcendentalist, tax resister, philosopher..." began the About section of the profile. Saunders liked the use of the first person, as if Thoreau filled out the profile himself. The profile picture was the same image he had seen before, and the only image of Thoreau in existence it seemed, showing him to be a slim guy with a long neck and frizzy brown beard. Next to the photograph, there was a quote from "Civil Disobedience" that said, *Let your life be a counter friction to stop the machine.*

It was a quote he'd used in one of his classes for their discussion of Thoreau. He clicked on the profile, then opened up the message he received along with the friend request. At least somebody was paying attention:

All men recognize the right of revolution; that is the right to refuse allegiance to and to resist the government, when its tyranny or its inefficiency are great and unendurable...

Nothing else was in the message—no signature, no acknowledgements, no specific link to anybody, though there did seem to be only one person likely to send him something like this.

"Who is this?" he wrote back, then pulled Anne Lamott's book, *Bird by Bird*, off his shelf, looking for inspiration about how to write his suicide note. This time he planned to get it done.

The First draft is the child's draft, where you let it all pour out and then let it romp all over the place, knowing that no one is going to see it and that you can shape it later.

Lamott's section on "shitty first drafts." How much could he really revise a suicide note?

It's not like you don't have a choice, because you do—you can either type or kill yourself.

He gave himself ten minutes to free write a draft and then put down his pen; at the very least, he had settled on who to address it to.

Dear Students, I am ruined. I have no reason to live. Goodbye. Your prof, Berlin Saunders.

Too fucking crybaby. It reminded him of some of those *Dear World* notes he saw on the Internet. Who would've thought that a suicide note would take so much out of him? Maybe it'd be better if he waited until he was sober again.

While he sat there, another message came in just as obscure.

What is the price-current of an honest man and patriot to-day? They hesitate, and they regret, and sometimes they petition. But they do nothing in earnest and with effect. They will wait, well disposed, for others to remedy evil, that they may no longer have it to regret.

Though it was not meant to inspire him to write his suicide note, Saunders couldn't help but apply these words to his situation. Why *was* he hesitating? What was he waiting for?

Dear Henry, he wrote back, *thank you for the inspiring words. See you in class!*

He received another message, yet another quote, this time not from Thoreau, with a link to a picture.

It was in 1846 that a thin crack first began to affect the sound of the bell. The bell was repaired in 1846 and rang during a celebration of George Washington's birthday, but the bell cracked again and has not been rung since. No one knows why the bell cracked either time.

The liberty bell. As he suspected, it could only be from one person. But what did this have to do with Thoreau and why did Adam create a profile to send this to him? Saunders noted the coincidence that the first crack in the liberty bell took place only three years before Thoreau published his essay.

Someone really ought to fix that thing, ADAM! he replied.

Eventually, he forgot about the message and got back to the more important business of drafting his suicide note. After making a pot of coffee, he was able to sit still long enough to draft a long and incoherent shitty first draft that went on for pages, when a third message from Adam came in.

This time with a link to an article.

Liberty Bell to Be Moved...Again?
Associated Press
Philadelphia, PA

It has been only a decade since the bell found a permanent home, but sources from the Liberty Center in Philadelphia say they are planning yet another move—this time only temporary. It turns out the bell is not the only thing cracked—an inspection made late last year revealed damage to the roof of the center caused when a winter storm of heavy snow and ice broke several sections of glass above the entrance. City inspectors say the repairs will be made this spring after the final winter thaw when the Center will be shut down for two weeks for repairs.

Where will this icon of freedom be moving?

Well, it turns out, nobody is quite sure yet, but a number of things are in the works—officials in Philadelphia have proposed displaying the bell somewhere else in the city, while a recent proposal by the mayor, currently gaining the most ground, is for a 15-state tour of the nation, beginning next month, that would provide the Liberty Bell Center revenue to pay for the million dollar damage without straining Pennsylvania taxpayers.

The last time the bell toured the nation was in 1903 making celebratory stops en route to Charleston, Massachusetts for the 128th anniversary of Bunker Hill. If the mayor gets his way, it will be the first time in a hundred years the bell will take to the road.

Field trip? Saunders wrote back, before reviewing his suicide note.

It was a shitty draft all right. *A shitty first draft for a shitty life.* He wondered if Lamott had a follow-up chapter for the completely hopeless second draft.

The second draft is the up draft, you fix it up.

This was about the only advice he was able to find from her.

Fix it up?

He felt more like giving it up.

At least for now.

He thought of one of his all-time favorite short stories,

"A Perfect Day for Bananafish" by J.D. Salinger. Seymour Glass had done it with a gun to his right temple while his shallow wife lay on the hotel bed without his even bothering to write a shitty first draft or note at all. They were all bananafish, weren't they? The Crawfords, the Stones, the Tom Coronas, grown too fat inside the academic hole. He may not have been them anymore, but he wasn't Seymour Glass either. Seymour had just returned from WWII, left hopeless by the atrocities he'd seen in Germany.

Dear Students, This life has been nothing but a shitty first draft, with no time for revision.

It was amazing what you could do when you finally let every-thing go. And when he woke up the next morning and looked at the work he'd done, he saw it clearly. It made him think of how Ezra Pound's "In a Station of the Metro" had been hundreds of lines long before he had cut it down to two simple lines. What else was there to say? The note captured everything. He could finally do it.

MIDTERM

CHAPTER 21
REQUIRED TEXTS

Was the gunman still out there? With only his thoughts to entertain him now, Berlin Saunders felt like an abandoned marionette playing dead on the classroom floor. He might've escaped if his limbs hadn't fallen asleep. It reminded him of the time he got his first and only tattoo on the inside of his left arm with some birthday money when he was eighteen. Having finished the job, the tattoo artist invited him to look in the mirror to see the work he'd done. Saunders jumped to his feet, forgetting he spent the past hour holding still, and collapsed to the floor. Embarrassed, he tried to get up only to realize both his arms had also gone numb. The tattoo artist and a waiting customer lifted him up by his shoulders and helped him take baby steps over to the mirror.

The tattoo was of an ignited wick coming out the top of the world, as if the earth itself were about to explode. Inevitably, when he wore short sleeves to school, his students would ask about it.

Claudia Clement, a French teacher, who once shared an office with Kathy, ran into Saunders at the supermarket just after their split, and was shocked by the tattoo peeking out from under his shirtsleeve.

"What does it mean?" she asked.

Without waiting for an answer, and unable to comprehend why anyone would have such a cynical image (which Saunders considered very un-French of her) permanently inked on his arm, she suggested it might serve as a political message about global warming.

You bet, Saunders wanted to tell her before walking away, Call me Al fuckin' Gore.

"Hmm…" was all he really managed to spit out. He often used this response when his students gave him dumb answers in class and he was too lazy or uninterested to refute them. The truth was, for the whole time he was with Kathy, he had been embarrassed by the already fading world exploding on his arm. Kathy thought it juvenile. Which it was.

"Good thing you wear a blazer to work," she once told him.

Saunders felt his phone vibrate in his pants pocket. A text message. Since he had been lying on the classroom floor, he heard other phones vibrating in the backpacks of his students. How many were dead? How many shots had he heard? In the chaos of the moment, he couldn't recall. But he didn't want to think too much about his students. To do so would make him feel a great responsibility to act. At least he still had enough sensation in his leg to feel the vibration. But who would be contacting him in the midst of this? And where were his rescuers? Where was the SWAT team, the Long Beach Police Department, the FBI? Hadn't they prepared for this? Surely, the media was all over it by now. Were the police planning on coming and saving him anytime soon? Everything was so quiet inside and outside the classroom. He longed for sirens, or at the very least, the sound of a news helicopter flying overhead.

What if it was the SWAT team sending him the text message,

telling him to stay put, or to get out, or to just keep playing dead? The suspense of finding out who texted him was growing bigger than the possibility of eternal darkness. But what if the gunman walked in just as he reached for his phone? The phone vibrated a second time to remind him there was a message waiting. He ran through the possibilities of who it might be. Was it worth risking his life? But once he'd felt the vibration, he couldn't stop thinking about it. The anticipation would kill him if the gunman didn't. So without opening his eyes, Saunders slowly began trying to move his fingers. Because of the way he landed, his arm had been left twisted, the palm of his hand facing upward, making the position of his body more likely to fool a suspicious mass murderer, but creating a problem for checking his text messages.

He felt the familiar pins as his fingers came back to life. Better to die than to obsess. What if the message were an important one that might save him? Eventually, as his whole hand regained circulation, he slipped it in his pocket. Why hadn't he thought of using his phone earlier to call for help?

In the midst of sliding his phone out, he thought he heard movement inside the classroom and he froze, afraid to look. Lying facedown on the carpet, for however long, had left him disoriented. Maybe it wasn't worth it. But then he felt the vibration yet again. And he couldn't resist. He waited and when the noise didn't repeat, opened his eyes, refusing to look anywhere else but at his phone:

Hi Berlin. Just wondering if you had a chance to read my manuscript?

The message was from Rich Hamlin, one of the three adjuncts he worked with who he knew from grad school. Obviously, Rich wasn't teaching today and had no idea what was happening. Saunders had been avoiding him all semester, after Rich cornered him one morning in the mailroom begging him to read his novel about a bizarre love triangle between a Western academic couple and the Muslim sex slave they try to rescue.

"Hmm..." was how Saunders had responded. The next day when he came in, however, the manuscript was lying in his box with a post-it note that said "no hurry" and a smiley face.

So much for the SWAT team. Who was going to rescue him from Rich Hamlin? He knew he should've declined when asked to give his phone information for the staff directory that year. What did it matter now though? He could be dead any minute. He didn't even have anyone to send a sappy farewell message to. He looked at the last text he ever sent Kathy. It was just a few weeks before Christmas break, and a few days before she left him: *You forced my finger into your asshole last night.*

Saunders couldn't help but play dead with a smile now.

Maybe he would reply to Rich Hamlin telling him what he *really* thought of his stupid novel. What did he have to lose? Instead, he sent another message, one perhaps just as brutal: *GET HELP!* He figured this was the one day in his life he could say this to someone and be completely vindicated.

CHAPTER 22

RULES FOR WRITERS

"For six months, I was in the hospital," Adam said. "Both my arms and legs in casts. Strung up like a puppet."

When Adam asked to meet with him during the eighth week of the semester, it had been Saunders who suggested the coffee shop by his apartment called The Library. Not only was it convenient, he also liked the name of the place—even if the coffee tasted like soot, and despite its name, there weren't any books.

"The physical pain was the least of my worries," Adam said. "It was all that time to think. And read. But I wanted to be back in the action."

Saunders placed a cigarette in his mouth and borrowed Adam's lighter. His eye twitched. Across the street, a woman and her two small children came out of the pet store with a pit bull that was wearing a humiliating red bow. All was at peace on the street that afternoon. A street where mothers and children took their pets to get washed and humiliated. A street on which you might wander with a lover.

"A lot of guys I grew up with," Adam said, "can't find a job. Their wives have left them. And maybe those are some of the luckier ones."

"What about you?" Saunders said.

"I'm all right," Adam said. "Thank god for the G.I. Bill."

"You mean that government handout?" he said, winking at Adam.

"Touché," Adam said. "The taxpayers pay both our salaries. But I'm not planning on taking advantage of the system much longer, sir. I don't feel like I have much of a future."

Well, that was one thing they had in common.

"I'd really be wasting taxpayers' money if I just sit in a classroom and do nothing with my life," Adam said.

"Works for me," Saunders said. "You're a damn good writer, Adam. Put it to use."

Adam looked away as if shy about it.

"So what happened with your girlfriend?" Saunders asked.

A pigeon walked beneath his chair and Saunders stomped at it so that it turned and started marching in the other direction.

"I don't know," Adam said. "Maybe I was too obsessed. Too hyper after I got back from the war. Love is addicting you know. Well, you know."

Of course, Saunders didn't really. It wasn't post-traumatic stress disorder that caused Kathy to dump him. It was that she couldn't stand him anymore. Or he couldn't stand her? Or they couldn't stand each other? Or what was it? Even now, he wasn't exactly sure—had they just drifted? Clearly, she had. Was it his lack of ambition that had finally done them in? When she'd thrown the glass of wine at his shirt, had it merely been symptomatic of an anger building for a long time? Certainly, four of their five years together had been happy. Why was it only the bad stuff that stuck in his head? Had he blocked out all the good memories?

"What about family?"

"My mom's still back home," Adam said. "She's older than you might think. Had me when she was 36. Also, an alcoholic. I mostly just send her cigarettes. Anything else?"

Saunders thought about it for a minute.

"Yes," he said. "Why me? What's so important you needed to meet me here?"

"It was something you said in class," Adam told him.

"I say a lot of things in class...," Saunders said. *That I don't mean.*

"You said the action a man takes isn't necessarily for the present moment, but for the future."

"I was paraphrasing Thoreau," Saunders said. "It was part of the lesson that day."

"So you didn't mean it then?" Adam asked.

"Of course I did," Saunders said.

Did he?

"Good," Adam said, reaching down into his camouflage bag that he'd set next to his seat and pulling it up on his lap, then unzipping the front pocket.

He dropped a card on the table and pushed it across the table next to Saunders's coffee cup.

"Do you know what that is?" Adam asked, leaning forward in his seat and grabbing the lighter off the table.

Saunders looked at the card.

"Not really. But I can guess."

"It's called a ROE card," Adam said. "Rules of Engagement. They issued it to every soldier in Iraq."

Saunders slid the card up off the table and into his hand. He already wanted another cigarette. The smell of Adam's freshly lit one was enticing him. To hell with it. He could chain smoke all he wanted now that he wasn't long for this world.

1. You may engage the following individuals based on their conduct:

a. Persons who are committing hostile acts against CF.

b. Persons who are exhibiting hostile intent towards CF.

"What's CF?" he asked.

"Coalition Forces," Adam said. "The bigger the threat, the more vicious we were allowed to be. But it got to a point where the size of the threat didn't matter anymore."

Saunders read on.

2. These persons may be engaged subject to the following instructions:

a. Positive Identification (PID) is required prior to engagement. PID is a reasonable certainty that the proposed target is a legitimate military target. If not PID, contact the next commander in line for decision.

b. Use Graduated Measure of Force. When time and circumstance permit, use the following degrees of graduated force when responding to hostile act/intent: (1) shout verbal warning to halt; (2) show your weapon and demonstrate intent to use it; (3) block access or detain; (4) fire a warning shot; (5) shoot to eliminate threat.

"Looks like there are just as many rules for war as there are for writing," Saunders said, picking up Adam's lighter.

"Except nobody abides by them in war," Adam said.

"Not so much in writing either," Saunders said.

It was that time of the afternoon when the marine layer began to come in, and the wind picked up, cooling down his coffee too much before he'd even drank the sludge.

Insurgent. PID. Graduated Measure of Force. Engage. WAC. SLOs. WTF. GWAR. This was the language of an institution, with its cold euphemisms and silly acronyms.

"Read the top," Adam said.

Saunders looked at the large bold print there.

NOTHING ON THIS CARD PREVENTS YOU FROM USING NECESSARY AND PROPORTIONAL FORCE TO DEFEND YOURSELF.

"It's time we defend ourselves, Professor Saunders. It's time to play by their own rules."

Saunders laughed.

"We? What do I have to defend myself against?" he said. "The insurgents in the Humanities?"

"We need to take action now. For the future."

"I thought you had no future," Saunders said.

"Doesn't mean I don't want one for other people. Shit's bad out there. This is my chance to do something meaningful. But I need you. Without you, I'll just be another loner weirdo. You establish credibility," Adam said. "Isn't that one of the first rules of making an argument? People respect you. You're educated. I'm just some army grunt no one will take seriously."

"You think too highly of me, Adam," Saunders said. "There's

nobody this country respects less than teachers. I'm an English professor. Not even that. I'm an *adjunct* instructor. Do you know what the word 'adjunct' means? It means *a thing added to something else as a supplementary rather than essential part.* I looked it up once."

"Well, if they look down on you as much as they do me, you're never going to be part of their club. They're using you just like they used me. Really, you're not much different than a soldier," Adam said. "And it sounds like you're making your own argument. It's time we make ourselves essential."

"I haven't experienced what you have," Saunders said. "And I've never been good at taking much action in my life. But if you want to protest the Liberty Bell, protest the Liberty Bell. It's not for me to stop you."

"Who said anything about protesting?" Adam said.

"What then?"

"I want to steal it," Adam said.

"You want to steal the Liberty Bell?" Saunders asked.

"And demand the crack be fixed. Something like that," Adam said. "Still working out the details."

"You're crazy," Saunders said, laughing.

"But you know there's another reason I asked for your help," Adam said, "...something more important."

"What's that?"

"You know what it's like to lose something."

Was it that he knew what it was like to lose something or that he had nothing to lose?

"Ah," Saunders said. "Breaking up with a girl is hardly on the level—"

"I'm not talking about that," Adam said.

"Then what are you talking about?" Saunders said.

"Your father."

"But steal the Liberty Bell?" Saunders said.

"You're an English teacher. Think of the symbolism."

And yet he couldn't help but feel flattered that Adam had thought he was radical enough to participate in such a plot. Which, of course, he wasn't.

There were huge obstacles to be dealt with in Adam's plot. 2000 pounds worth of obstacles. This was the weight of the Liberty Bell. No way they could move it. But why was he even thinking about?

"That's totally irrational," Saunders said.

"But isn't that the kind of vision that made this nation great? Without it, we wouldn't have gone to the moon. Certainly, going to the moon was not rational," Adam said.

"We wouldn't have gone to the moon if a few smart guys hadn't stayed in school," Saunders said. "You've got a whole life ahead of you. Why go to jail for something like this?"

"A whole life to do what?" Adam said. "Wallow in a miserable 9 to 5 job and wait for cancer to kill me? How many lives do you know that are essential?"

. . . the greatest madness a man can commit in this life is to let himself die without anybody killing him or any other hands ending his life except those of melancholy.

He had read this in *Don Quixote* just that morning.

"Though I have to warn you," Adam said. "It could be a suicide mission."

CHAPTER 23

ESTABLISHING AUTHORITY

It'd been a few weeks since he'd run into Tom in the mailroom. But unlike his usual garb, Tom was dressed up in a suit and had a heavy dose of some kind of peppery cologne on that made Saunders sneeze four times when he entered. He had a bunch of notecards in his hand and he was standing in front of the mailboxes flipping through them.

"What's the occasion?" Saunders asked Tom, who could hardly contain his nervous excitement.

"Don't you know?" he said. "They're interviewing for the WAC job today and guess who got the call?"

"So, your efforts have paid off? I'm not surprised," Saunders said. "You're perfectly qualified."

"I'm one class down this semester," Tom said. "Lost it at my other school to a full-timer. I need to get this."

How small Tom's dream seemed. Saunders thought back to his own futile attempts at getting a full-time position and how important it all seemed and how devastating the rejections had been. Ten applications, ten failures. Soul crushing. Humiliating. Twice he received the form email from the colleges he worked at without even being granted an interview.

Dear Berlin Saunders,

On behalf of the selection committee, I would like to thank you for taking the time to apply for the English instructor position at said-college-you've-loyally-worked-at-for-years. It is with regret that I inform you…

Sincerely, chair-who-hired-you, Ph.D.

And all for what? A job no one respected at a school that couldn't afford to even pay for a DVD player in every classroom? Maybe Adam was right. Maybe it was time to make his life *essential*. But how? Certainly not by trying to steal the Liberty Bell. Though he had to applaud the gall of that kid. Maybe when you've been shot at a bunch of times, other things seemed less scary.

"The last time I saw you, you were on a stretcher with fake blood on your shirt. Great performance, by the way," Saunders said.

Tom put his finger to his lips as if to warn Saunders and then Saunders heard the snoring once again coming from the desk by the copy machine. Habits develop quickly.

"Don't worry," Saunders whispered, "he can't even hear himself."

"Seriously," Tom said, annoyed.

"Maybe they should provide cots for adjuncts," Saunders said.

Tom didn't seem to have much sympathy. He was already projecting himself as a full-timer. Saunders wondered if Tom would still talk to him if he did get hired. Of course, they were never going to hire Tom as a full-time professor.

"I still want that bag you know," Tom said, gesturing to Saunders's torn leather bag he'd set in front of the mailboxes.

What was this obsession? The bag had holes in the bottom.

"By the way," Saunders said, changing the subject. "Whatever happened with your plagiarists?"

"Which one?" Tom said. "Caught a bunch more already."

He got this crazed and proud look on his face and suddenly Saunders saw it. Up until that moment, he hadn't realized it, but somewhere in Tom was a failed cop. It was a look he'd recognized in many of his colleagues, but had never placed what it was. The love affair with authority. Albeit, a tiny morsel of authority, but you took what you could get.

"The first students got expelled," Tom said. "For straight up stealing. But now I'm working on three others: one guy who just doesn't know how to use signal phrases, one girl who was 'just getting help from somebody' and never came back, and then another guy who according to Copycat.com turned in an almost identical paper in another class."

Saunders got his B.A. without ever including a works cited page on any of his papers. And when had giving your paper to someone to proofread become a crime? Not to mention how often he turned in the same paper to multiple professors during his college career, sometimes tweaking it, sometimes turning it in as is, hopefully remembering to change the date which, he had to admit, did piss him off the few times students had forgotten to at least do that. He had even used the same vague title, over and over again: "Unknown Stations." He couldn't even remember why he used it in the first place and had no idea what it meant except that it created a mystery that could fill in for anything. All he ever had to do was add whatever subtitle he wished: "Unknown Stations: The Search for Meaning in Samuel Beckett's *Waiting for Godot*."

"Unknown Stations: How America Botched the Response to 9/11." "Unknown Stations: Hamlet's Inner Chernobyl."

"Unknown Stations: Freire and the Pedagogy of Revolution."

Yes, the pedagogy of revolution. Could he be a revolutionary? Could he make Freire proud? What would Freire do? Freire would be disappointed in him. Wasn't the whole point of the composition classroom to turn students into revolutionaries? Had he not been successful? Maybe he was rejecting his true nature to be a revolutionary and he just didn't know it. And what if he did help Adam and they could get away with it? Could this be the start of a new career? And what would his new title be then? Domestic terrorist? *Adjunct* domestic terrorist?

"Whatever happened with your right-wing nut job?" Tom said as if reading his mind.

"Turns out he's one of the best writers in the class," Saunders said. "The guy's been to hell and back. Wrote a great narrative essay about his time in Iraq. I'm kinda jealous really. He writes better than I do. But I think he's a little unhinged."

"Aren't we all?" said Tom.

Despite everything, Saunders was still proud when his students turned in good work and felt like he deserved some bragging rights. Even for the ones with criminal intent.

"You didn't tell him he's great, did you?" Tom said.

"Of course not," Saunders said. "I mean, I encouraged him a little. But still red ink all over his paper naturally."

"You know it's also possible," Tom said, "you're just a good teacher. Have you told him about the scholarship? $1,000 for the best essay."

"He'd never submit," Saunders said. "He's shy about his writing."

Tom pulled out a flyer from his bag.

"Maybe you can inspire him," he said, handing Saunders the flyer.

English Department Best Essay Award
Deadline: Monday, April 15

* Entries should be submitted to the English Dept. office (printed on high-quality printers) by the deadline.

* Students may submit only one entry and must be enrolled in the spring semester to be eligible for this scholarship

"Who's on the committee?" Saunders asked, wondering if it'd be worthwhile to convince Adam to submit. After all, $1000 dollars of real-world money could be enough to convince him of his talent.

"I am," Tom said, looking around him, then putting a hand on Saunders's shoulder. "So tell me. How's everything else? How are you *really* holding up?"

A cop, after all. Cops were corrupt. Cops liked to get into everyone's business. Cops were nosy. Could one ever expect loyalty from a cop? Cops beat people up when they thought no one was looking.

"Everything's great," Saunders said.

"Really?" Tom said.

He had no reasonable assurance of Tom's sincerity just like he had no reasonable assurance that he'd have a job next semester, which was the reason he could collect unemployment in the state of California over summer break.

"*Really,*" Saunders said.

CHAPTER 24
The Love Song Of J. Adjunct Saunders

"Okay everyone," said Saunders, "today we're going to talk about a poem and I know how you all feel about poems, but I don't care."

Saunders had brought copies of Whitman's "When I Heard the Learn'd Astronomer," which he passed out to the class.

When I heard the learn'd astronomer,
When the proofs, the figures, were ranged in columns before me,
When I was shown the charts and diagrams, to add, divide,
   and measure them,
When I sitting heard the astronomer where he lectured with
   much applause in the lecture-room,
How soon unaccountable I became tired and sick,
Till rising and gliding out I wander'd off by myself,
In the mystical moist night-air, and from time to time,
Look'd up in perfect silence at the stars.

It was poetry, which meant literature, which meant forbidden, but he didn't care about that either. The students moaned. Their experience with poetry had been tainted long ago in their high school English classes, or by a chance night walking into some coffee shop where a reading was taking place. Not even Walt Whitman could save them.

"What is your impression of this poem?" he asked the class, hardly giving them time to think about it. "Why does the narrator reject the lecture he's attended?"

Nobody said anything. Then Justin Keneficke raised his hand and said,

"I don't really understand what's going on."

It was honest at least.

"Who is this 'learn'd astronomer'?" Saunders said. "The narrator has attended some kind of lecture, hasn't he? A lecture by an astronomer. What's significant about that? Are there any details he gives us? What is he saying about all those 'proofs and figures and arrangements in columns'?"

When he looked around the room at these gray concrete walls, it was kind of the way he'd always imagined prison.

Adam raised his hand.

"Exactly that. They're just proofs, charts, and math, basically. Theoretical. Whereas the narrator completely rejects this by going outside and actually looking at the sky."

"But does he?" Saunders said. "I'm not sure he does entirely reject the lecture. Sure, it's just information. The astronomer is giving facts and figures to explain everything, but the narrator also refers to himself as unaccountable."

It didn't take much thinking. Just the script he'd used in previous classes.

"But who is unaccountable?" Adam said. "The man in the room talking about the stars or the man who actually goes out and looks at them and makes up his own mind?"

He didn't know the answer. All he knew is that he'd never been accountable for very much in his life.

"No doubt that's the most common way to interpret it," Saunders said. "You have an 'educated' man in the room talking about the stars, and then you have the poet, the man of action, who leaves that room to go out and actually look up at the stars."

"Yes," Adam said. "Though I don't think it matters that he's a poet. It matters that he decides things for himself."

"But maybe that is part of the anti-intellectual sentiment that is so problematic in this country," Saunders said. "People always ignoring the facts and deciding things for themselves. Do facts matter?"

"Facts matter," Adam said. "But at the same time, they don't. At some point, you have to make a decision about the world."

"Sometimes, knowledge of the facts can make things more incredible," Saunders said.

Tess Mackenzie raised her hand.

"God didn't make the stars intending us to fact check them," she said.

Thanks for your contribution, Tess.

"I think the point is that facts change," Adam said.

"Not always," Saunders said. "The world will never be flat again, will it?"

"It's possible," Adam said.

"No, it isn't," Saunders said. "We've been in space. We've seen the round world."

"Maybe we'll learn something new about reality," Adam said. "And suddenly what we thought was a solid thesis will turn out not to be."

"If you believe that we've actually been to space," Vanessa

Rivas said. "It's possible the government lied to us about that, too. I don't think we went to the moon."

"Conspiracies rely entirely on the obfuscation of facts," Saunders said.

Nobody knew what that word meant. But nobody asked. And he didn't bother explaining it to them.

"Conspiracies rely on something more incredible than even the obscuring of facts," Saunders said. "They rely on massive organization and secrecy."

"Sometimes it matters more what we see with our own eyes," Adam said. "Our personal experience. You can't teach that. Which is why I don't think it matters that he's a poet. What matters is that he trusts himself just like Emerson would tell him to."

"Still, one might argue if it hadn't been for his attending the lecture in the first place, it's possible he might not have looked at the stars at all. How can we assume he would?"

"I don't think that's the point at all," Adam said. "I think he knows it's bullshit. It makes him tired and sick."

"And unaccountable," Saunders said.

"But it's unclear on that point," Adam said. "What's the 'unaccountable' referring to? Him or to the lecture?"

Adam was like the narrator in Whitman's poem. He preferred to see the stars rather than talk about them whereas, in all truth, Saunders hadn't looked up at the sky in a long time. *Do I dare disturb the universe?* He had moved from Whitman to Eliot. Had the theme of this class been different, he'd have gone over "The Love Song of J. Alfred Prufrock" like he did a few semesters before in a beginning literature course he taught, themed "The Outsider." Was he not Prufrock after all? Did he dare disturb the foundation between action and inaction? He had always loved the lyricism of that poem. But since his first reading in his early twenties, he had recently come to change his mind about it. Prufrock was beginning to hit a little too close to home. Even the last time he had taught it, it had humiliated him when his students laughed at the poem.

"Eat the peach, dude," one of his students said.

He had tried to plead with them that it was a great poem and that Eliot was a great poet, but eventually gave up. He could no longer make them understand. Just like how he had tried to plead with Kathy, at first, but had also given up. He could no longer make her understand either. She had left him for another man. His boss.

And what would she say if he killed himself? *Do I dare disturb the university?* Hadn't she always complained that he never followed through on anything? Like the way he'd leave dishes in the sink for days after she cooked something. Though she loved to cook and was good at it, she couldn't help but see those symbolic undertones of oppression in the kitchen while he was off reading in the other room. He never wanted her in the kitchen. He just didn't know how to cook and often offered to take them out.

"No," she'd say, frustrated. "I'll just do it."

He always offered to wash the dishes, but sometimes, was too stuffed or drunk, and would promise to get them the next morning. But there had been times he hadn't followed through. *Crawford was probably the kind of guy who always followed through.* He probably even knew how to cook. But cooking had never made a man go down in history. Martin Luther King might have been a master chef. But nobody would ever know it.

What did any of these memories even matter anymore now that his world was ending? How had he come to prefer Eliot's poem "The Hollow Men" to "Prufrock" anyway. *This is the way the world ends/This is the way the worlds ends…*

And, if he played it right, it wouldn't be with a whimper either. But a bang.

CHAPTER 25
Subordination/Coordination

From: kstone@lbcc.edu

To: English-Faculty@lbcc.edu

Subject: Hooters

Attention Colleagues:

You may or may not have heard the horrifying news that athletic director Frank Seagull has chosen "Hooters" restaurant to be one of the official sponsors of this year's sporting events on campus. Many of us in the Humanities have called and left messages voicing our concerns, which have essentially been ignored by Frank and even more so, by the administrators who have allowed this to happen. For those of you who don't know "Hooters" (and why would you?), it is a sports bar that promotes the objectification of women, by asking its waitresses to wear scantily clad mid-riff tank tops and short shorts to wait on a mostly male clientele, thus, creating an inherently sexist environment, disgracing all the advances women have made towards equality in the last fifty years. This is not something the college should be allowing since its own policy specifically forbids any form of discrimination in regards to race, class, religion, or gender. What sort of message is this sending to our female students? Or worse, to our male ones?

In lieu of having not received a response from Frank or any administrators about this issue, the Humanities faculty are working on scheduling a rally in front of the president's office next week. We hope you'll join us in this effort to promote a fair and equal college culture. I will be putting flyers in all of your boxes and we'll be having a sign-making potluck the night before the protest in Humanities 312. More information to come. Thank you for your attention, and we hope you join us!

Sincerely,
Professor Katherine Stone

"A woman reading Playboy feels a little like a Jew reading a Nazi manual."
-Gloria Steinem

CHAPTER 26

ORAL PRESENTATIONS

Saunders forgot all about it being St. Patrick's Day when he swung open the doors of 3636. It was Monday, and he'd brought his copy of *Don Quixote* hoping for a quiet empty bar. He'd done most of his drinking at home lately and had managed to read quite a bit of the second part.

Instead of an empty bar though, he was welcomed by a packed one, with a sticky mess of spilled shots, a loud and obnoxious crowd, and a bartender, Phil, drunk and wearing a leprechaun hat and green beaded necklace.

"Professor Saunders!" Phil yelled, putting one hand down on the bar to balance himself. "Thought you left these parts for somewhere more sophisticated."

Phil reached down into a box behind the bar and handed Saunders the same green beads he was wearing. He set down a beer and, next to it, a shot of Jameson, then noticed the book in Saunders's hand.

"A professor even on St. Patty's," he said.

Without anywhere to sit, Saunders placed the beads in his blazer pocket and stood alone next to the edge of the bar, by the front window. He hated St. Patrick's Day. Amateur hour, of course. And wasn't Patrick just some fourth century ignoramus missionary who Christianized a nation that didn't need Christianizing? Detestable both in legend (banning snakes, etc.) and in reality (colonizing the masses) topped off by the cheap commercialism of shamrocks, leprechauns, and green beer. Even the Irish hated the holiday. And yet, for some reason, Saunders's fellow Americans loved it. Even the tiniest drop of Irish blood made his people go insane on St. Patrick's Day. The holiday had turned into a celebration of, not Catholicism, but all things Irish. He had nothing against the Irish. Except maybe Bono. But everyone hated Bono.

Phil rang the bar bell and paused the jukebox.

"Attention everyone," he said.

He held up his shot of whiskey and toasted all the patrons in the bar.

"To your mother's children," he shouted. "Happy St. Patty's Day, motherfuckers!" Saunders downed his shot then took a sip of his beer. He peeked through the blinds out onto the street. A few late-night stragglers walked their dogs past the bar. Often, when he'd been standing in front smoking a cigarette, sometimes even when it was still light out, joggers would run by and on a couple weekday afternoons, he'd even run into people he knew, including one time a girl from high school who just happened to live in the neighborhood.

He felt a pinch through his blazer on the back of his arm and turned around to catch a whiff of strong perfume that burned his nose like a fresh bite of Wasabi. On the other end of it was a curvy Latina with blonde streaks in her black hair, wearing a sleeveless green dress with large hoop earrings and the same green beads hanging down across her perky breasts.

"He made me do it, Teacher," she said.

Saunders looked to Phil who winked and signaled them both over. He had three more shots of Jameson lined up. Saunders grabbed one and the girl grabbed the other.

"To your mother's children," Phil said, "and to your children's mother." The whiskey burned, though less so than the woman's perfume. He finished the last sip of his first beer and found himself ordering another one. Phil may have been his friend, but he was also a damned good bartender and knew how to make his patrons stay.

"So what do you teach, Teacher?"

A young pretty face, her age indeterminate, probably somewhere in her thirties.

"English," he said.

"Oh, I love English!" she said. "So no green tonight or what, Teacher?"

He quickly began to despise the way she called him "teacher." Saunders reached into his blazer pocket, pulled out his beads, and held them up to her. She grabbed them from his hand and put them over his head like a medal of dishonor.

"Much better, Teacher," she said. She stuck out her hand to introduce herself.

"I'm Liz, by the way," she said.

There was something sexy about her accent, but he wasn't any good at small talk.

"I like your Irish beard, Teacher," she said. She put her hand under his chin and scratched the red hair mixed in with the increasingly white ones. This embarrassed him and he became so awkward that she eventually gave up and went to talk to another man, a regular who fixed Porsches at a dealership somewhere nearby.

After she left, Saunders went to take a piss, then headed back toward his safe space by the window where he'd left his cigarettes with his book, almost walking right into a tall twenty-something redhead. She was about to excuse herself but stopped when she recognized him.

"Wait a minute," she said. "You were my English professor."

He looked a little more closely, his eyes fading with each sip of booze he drank. He recognized her now. It was Nicole Ferguson with those gorgeous big brown eyes and long thin neck who he had lusted after for fifteen weeks in both mind and body a few semesters ago.

"You don't remember me," she said.

He surely did. Oh, yes, did he ever. Though he forgot most of his students, he rarely forgot the attractive ones. But he couldn't let her know. She had changed her hair color, grown a couple semesters older.

How could he forget Nicole Ferguson? Not quite in the honeymoon phase of his relationship with Kathy, but in the sulking middle, there had been fantasies about Nicole. Still, he would never have considered anything back then. For better or worse, he was all Kathy's. Those years had been productive years. He wrote essays, tried his hand at a few new poems (the first he'd written since grad school), and constantly searched the higheredjobs.com website for full-time tenure track jobs. At the time, his lusting after Nicole Ferguson had always involved some permissive ménage-a-trois fantasy with Kathy to absolve him of his guilt.

"I still remember your class," she said. "It was one of my favorites." He felt embarrassed, the way he imagined famous artists, writers, or, eh, rock stars felt when fans came up and praised them all the time.

"We read great stuff in there," she continued.

"Cigarette?" he said, not knowing what else to say. How long had he been there? The booze had hit him.

"I don't really smoke," she said, "but I'll keep you company."

Once outside, she said, "I majored in English because of your class, by the way."

"I'm so sorry to ruin your life like that," he joked, making her laugh, as she took a drag of his cigarette anyway, and coughed out un-inhaled smoke.

"Don't be," she said, "A part-time job at Barnes and Noble is what I always wanted."

They laughed together. He told her that reminded him of the six years in his early twenties he'd spent working at a Borders bookstore.

"I drove by there the other day," he said. "They turned it into an Urgent Care."

"That seems appropriate."

She had a sense of humor, which he admired. It reminded him of the early days with Kathy, before everything turned so hostile between them.

He'd never successfully hit on a student before and he didn't have much hope of it happening now.

"Those beads are a nice touch with the blazer, by the way," she said.

Saunders had forgotten about the beads and felt embarrassed. He ripped them over his neck and put them back in his pocket.

"Wasn't my idea," he said.

Once he finished the cigarette, he felt reluctant to go back in. With the only peace and quiet to be found outside, he knew they wouldn't be able to hear each other in there. He was just about to light up another smoke to stall the moment, when Liz peeked out the door and called to him.

"Teacher," she said. "Phil says to come inside for another shot."

"Tell him I'll be there in a minute."

"You're pretty popular, *teacher*," Nicole said, denying his offer of a cigarette, as he lit his own.

"I met her like five minutes ago," he said. "How about you? Who'd you come with?"

"Just some friends inside," she said.

"Listen," he said, pacing a little as he tried to ask. "Do you want to get out of here for a bit? Take a walk. Would your friends be pissed?"

"Where do you want to go?" she asked.

He hadn't thought that far ahead. The beach was only two blocks from them and Saunders couldn't remember the last time he walked down there. It was an option anyway. Even if they just walked around the neighborhood. What were the chances of running into her again? Soon he'd be a dead man. The least he could do was try.

"Anywhere that they won't have green beer," Saunders said.

She smiled.

"Sure," she said. "Let me just tell my friends inside I'll be back."

Had it all been too easy? He couldn't remember the last time he'd been so bold. If ever. Anyway, they were just going for a walk. She only saw him as her English teacher. It made him feel guilty that he was even entertaining the thought of sleeping with her. Teachers weren't supposed to have a life outside of the classroom, much less a *sex* life. Despite that, the culture at large loved to portray two types of teachers—the ones who were hot and you wanted to fuck and the ones so nerdy and ugly no one wanted to fuck. Teachers were allowed to be sex objects but criticized when they wanted to have sex. Teachers were not even supposed to be asexual, but u*n-sexual.*

Nicole returned and suggested they stay close by walking around the neighborhood. Just as they started down the street, he heard that voice again.

"Teacher!"

Footsteps came clicking up behind him. He wanted to ignore them and pick up his pace, but it was impossible.

"Teacher!"

Oh, what was it now? Finally, he turned around and there was Liz.

"You forgot something, Teacher," she said, handing him his copy of *Don Quixote.* Surprised he had forgotten about his book, he took it from her hands and thanked her.

"No problem, Teacher," she said, winking at him. "See you around."

Saunders shoved the thick book into his blazer pocket so hard that he tore the seam of it, but it didn't matter, because his mind was somewhere else.

The night was warm and loud as they walked past the other bars on Broadway Avenue. Nicole talked during the whole walk, told him she'd be graduating in a couple months and was waiting to hear back from Ph.D. programs in English. He wanted to stop her, to cut her off, to tell her it wasn't worth it, that it would ruin her love of life forever, but he wanted to kiss her more.

"Okay, your turn," she said. "Give it to me. What's your story? Why are you in 3636 on a school night, with a book, wearing a blazer?"

"What can I say?" Saunders said. "As someone recently told me, I'm a nerd."

"Doesn't take an English major to figure that one out. So what else?"

"What else do you want to know?"

"Do you eat GMOs?" she said. "Are you Democrat or Republican? What's your favorite color? Your favorite bird? I realize I know nothing about you except that you think it's okay to use the first person in an academic essay. Oh, and you're an easy grader."

When she spoke, her words were rushed. She felt as awkward as he did. Saunders could feel her brain nervously ticking inside her skull, attempting to size him up and analyzing the whole moment as they walked down Newport Avenue, past million-dollar nuclear family California bungalows with TVs flickering in the living room and kitchen lights left on.

"How about this?" she said. "What's your favorite book? I mean you were my English *teacher*."

"Good question about the book," Saunders told her. "My favorite book. What's my favorite book? Well, as you know with any reader, there isn't just one. What's yours?"

"I asked you first."

"Okay, fine," Saunders said. "I'd have to go with *Moby Dick*."

"Of course, you do," she said. "Such a man's book!"

"I know," he said. "A lot of people hate it."

"On the contrary," she said, "I love it. But I'm kind of a man about the books I read, that's all. I can't read all that girly shit. Jane Austen and crap. Makes me want to puke."

They turned up another street with more houses, more televisions flickering in windows, more kitchen lights on. Saunders glanced in the windows as he walked by.

"Any pets?"

"Nope."

"Kids?"

"No."

"Wife? Girlfriend?"

"No."

"Hobbies?"

"None. I'm really starting to feel like a loser," Saunders said.

"Hobbies are for losers," Nicole said. "Hobbies just mean you're not really into anything. Plus, who's got time for them?"

They were practically in front of his apartment. Saunders didn't want their night to end and invited her upstairs; at that moment, he wanted to grab Nicole and kiss her, but he didn't. *There will be time…* Instead, he invited her in.

He couldn't remember the last time he'd had company and realized he wasn't prepared. All the booze in the apartment he had drunk already, the only water was from the sink, and the apartment smelled like sour milk from a bowl of cereal he'd left in the sink for at least a week. It was the first time he'd entered his apartment as a stranger would and realized he had been negligent about cleaning anything since Kathy moved out. But the worst part was the memories everywhere. What was he thinking inviting her up there? Every remnant began to present itself. Even a refrigerator magnet held a picture of them at Thanksgiving, stuck up there, which he quickly shoved in a kitchen drawer. Had he been staring at this picture for all these months? If so, he had done it unconsciously. The most revealing, to him anyway, were the bookshelves, with gaps everywhere, where his books had fallen down, in the spaces where Kathy had removed all of hers.

"Sorry, I didn't plan for any guests," he said.

He grabbed a few months' worth of junk mail that had started on the coffee table and eventually drifted on to the couch and carried it off to the trashcan. Along the way, he noticed another thing, that much of the mail still had Kathy's name on the envelope.

"To be honest," he said, "you're the first person who's been through that door in two months."

They sat down on the couch. Saunders managed to find two

beers in the refrigerator, one of which he had offered to her, though she declined and asked for water instead. She took a sip of the water, set it down on the coffee table, and put her hand on his chest. Then they kissed.

"Relax," she said.

She pushed him back against the couch and unzipped him. He couldn't believe this was happening.

Saunders put his head back and stared up at his bookshelves when he realized his copy of *Don Quixote* had been in his blazer pocket since the bar. Seconds later, he exploded.

She sat up and wiped her hand across her mouth, and when she did, it wasn't Nicole's face at all staring back at him, but Liz's. She reached for the water on the coffee table while Saunders zipped up. Liz smiled and then leaned up against him on the couch.

"Tell me, did I pass the class, Teacher?"

CHAPTER 27

Give Me Liberty Or Give Me . . . Debt?

Los Angeles Times

Bells are ringing! Or should we say, not ringing as Philadelphia braces for the opening ceremony of the 15-state Liberty Bell Tour, which kicks off tonight and ends in Los Angeles on May 12. The historical emblem will be transported right through our city, and tens of thousands of people are expected to line the streets for a view. This, of course, will involve shutting down routes all across the county. The inevitable disruption of weekday traffic is already being referred to as "Carpocalypse." An iconic symbol of American independence dating back to 1751 and one of the most important emblems of our democracy, the bell's cross-country journey promises to be a high security event the mayor has referred to as the "mother of all parades."

The bell's arrival in Los Angeles is still far away, as it leaves Philadelphia tonight on its 50-day tour that will take it through multiple states, stopping in 15, and passing through much of the American landscape, from National Parks to National Monuments (See Mt. Rushmore) to national playgrounds (its final stop before arriving in L.A. will be Las Vegas).

There has been some controversy, however. Some have expressed concern over the environmental impact of transporting the Bell across the country, noting that transport is the number one largest contributor to air pollution. In Washington, members of Congress are at odds with the state of Pennsylvania over the cost of the tour, as the tab will not be picked up entirely by the state, but by the nation. Further concerns include the fact that hauling the Liberty Bell across the country is an issue of National Security, and the cost of security alone is said to be higher than a presidential caravan if needed for 50 straight days. But, of course, the longest a president lasts is eight years, while the Liberty Bell has been with us for 250 years. Perhaps this proves, once again, that freedom isn't free.

CHAPTER 28
Summary/Response

At first, he could only hear the slight rumbling of something off in the distance. The room was quiet as his students were ending the class by writing in their journals. But gradually, the sound got louder and louder. Whatever it was, it was coming closer. A few students looked up from their papers. They were already distracted enough given this was the last class before spring break. Since the only windows were high above and covered with gray vinyl blinds, nobody could see out. For all he knew, a riot was going on and nobody told him about it. Vanessa Rivas got up from her seat as if to investigate, but instead, plugged her phone charger into the classroom wall socket.

Saunders peeked outside the door, but the hall was empty. Across the way, he could see the light on in another classroom. Business as usual. Or maybe like him, they didn't know what the fuck was going on. A voice on a megaphone. Some kind of call and response. The distant rumbling of a tom drum. He returned to his desk. More students looked up from their journals. Some set down their pens. He looked at the clock.

"Should we get under the desks?" Caitlyn Cotter asked. The class laughed. It did sound like an earthquake, if not for the voices growing more distinct as they got closer.

He heard a couple car horns off in the distance. Then all of the sudden, the sound got really loud. The monster had entered the building. His students put down their pens fast. He could hear marching on the staircase. Whoever was headed towards his classroom was chanting. He glanced at Adam who shrugged.

"Okay," Saunders said, "brace yourself for the apocalypse."

The students laughed.

Had he missed an email somewhere like the time he'd given an in-class essay during a scheduled fire drill? And more importantly, was this something he'd be able to excuse the class over?

Voices. What sounded like hundreds of voices filled the hallways. Saunders opened the classroom door again just as the herd came roaring past it. Dozens of colleagues, faces he recognized from meetings, or from walking around campus, or from the staff parking lot rushed past, stomping their feet, shouting, with signs that said, "SAY NO TO HOOTERS."

He heard a familiar voice on a megaphone that he couldn't quite place, urging them on like a general marching behind his cadets in boot camp.

"WHAT DO WE WANT?"

"ACTION!"

He remembered now the email from Kathy.

A short and fat little woman with blonde hair walked by with a sign that read, "NO ONE OBJECTIFIES ME." Sad, but true. One woman had cleverly punned the name to say SHOOTERS and drew a bullet firing into a heart with the word EQUALITY written inside it. Other adjuncts were opening their doors and looking outside their classrooms.

"WHAT DO WE WANT?" a voice repeated in the megaphone,

as the crowds came stampeding down the hall.

"EQUALITY," the crowd of protesters yelled in response.

"WHAT DO WE WANT?" the voice repeated.

"EQUALITY," they yelled again.

And it wasn't just the women. Men chanted alongside them in solidarity. One of the males even held up a sign that read, "THIS IS WHAT A FEMINIST LOOKS LIKE."

"WHAT ARE WE GOING TO GET?" the voice on the megaphone said once again.

A headache? Saunders thought.

"JUSTICE," the crowd shouted.

"WHAT DO WE WANT?"

He wanted a cigarette. A cigarette and some lunch. One more class to go. It was barely 11 o'clock, but he was already starving. Had he known he might have legitimately gotten out of class, he might have joined them. What the hell? Was it too late? He had nothing against Hooters, though he'd never been there. He did remember hearing they had good chicken wings. Those poor chickens. Nobody cared about the chickens. Nobody was marching for them. They also wanted equality. They just wanted to live. And they had breasts too, but instead of objectifying them, we ate them.

He imagined the faculty storming down the hallway as a bunch of chickens, protesting Hooters chicken wings.

"WHAT DO WE WANT?"

"TO LIVE!"

"WHAT ARE WE GOING TO GET?"

"DIPPED IN RANCH!"

Wasn't the faculty nothing but a bunch of chickens anyway? Who was he to talk, of course? He hadn't even been able to put the moves on his ex-student. Speaking of breasts. There he went again. This protest was making him hungry *and* horny. He couldn't help but think about breasts at the drop of the name Hooters. When he had hugged Nicole goodbye, he'd felt them press up against him. But he hadn't had the guts to do anything. He'd been too chicken and gone home with someone else.

"WHAT DO WE WANT?"

A blowjob.

"WHAT DO WE WANT?"

A full-time job.

There were so many other things the faculty could have been protesting.

He had heard the prices were a bit inflated over at Hooters anyway, to take advantage of the men who went there, but they weren't protesting prices.

"WHAT DO WE WANT?"

The megaphone got louder as the leader approached. The rest of the group reached the end of the hallway and were exiting out into the staircase on the other side.

"WHAT DO WE WANT?"

By then, he wanted hot wings, soaked in spicy buffalo sauce, price be damned.

He looked back at his students, who were all confused by the whole thing.

"Like, what are they protesting?" Romeo Flores asked.

"Hooters," Beverly MacDowell said. "You know, the restaurant?"

"Never heard of it," Justin Keneficke said.

"They make the girls dress like sluts," Vanessa Rivas said. "I guess."

"Awesome," Justin said. He was definitely going to be visiting Hooters soon.

"I read about it in the school paper," Vanessa said. "Something about the school getting Hooters to sponsor their sports team or something."

"I don't think it's a big deal," Jessica Suskind said. "I have a friend that works there. She likes it. She makes good tips."

And then he saw them.

One of the last to turn the corner. Crawford and Kathy coming down the hall. Saunders would have ducked inside the classroom except he hadn't been quick enough and made eye contact with Harry who nodded.

Dammit.

"WHAT DO WE WANT?" shouted the man into the bullhorn standing next to them, who was none other than Tom Corona. He gave Saunders a thumbs-up sign as they passed by.

"WHAT DO WE WANT?" he yelled.

"EQUALITY," the crowd repeated.

"WHAT ARE WE GOING TO GET?"

"RESPECT!"

Despite the distraction, Saunders was relieved when he looked up at the clock and saw that the march through the classroom hallways had sucked up the last ten minutes and he excused everyone. Only Adam lingered behind, slowly stuffing his folder into his backpack as the other students left.

"There are guys in my hometown who are addicted to drugs and can't find a job," he said, "but this is what the professors are concerned about. I'm afraid if we don't fix that crack soon, something worse will come."

How could Saunders argue?

"But it does give me hope," Adam said. "If you can get people upset enough about a sports bar with scantily-clad women, all we need to do is expose people to what's really going on in this country."

Saunders wasn't sure what was really going on in this country, but he knew there was a lot to be protesting. And maybe that's all his colleagues were trying to express, even if they'd picked the wrong target. Maybe they felt as powerless as he did about the disparity between full-time and part-time faculty, men and women, or the lack of benefits or retirement or job security. Maybe their anger had been misdirected at a restaurant that just wanted to offer men a little reprieve after a long workday, to eat chicken wings, watch a game, and objectify their waitress.

He locked up the classroom as he saw a couple of protesters, their signs down at their sides now, walking back through the hallway, probably on their way to class. There were still lessons to be taught, papers to grade, assignments to be given even if the whole world was going to shit because of Hooters.

"So, what's next?" Adam asked him.

"Chicken wings," Saunders said.

CHAPTER 29

MODELS FOR WRITERS

"This woman was walking towards them," Adam said, "with a bag in her hands. They didn't know what to do. They were scared…"

"Just the two of you?" the waitress interrupted. She wore a tight white tank top with an owl on it that said HOOTERS in orange letters across the front. Saunders never thought of it as that kind of "hooter" before. To match the shirt, the hostess wore orange short shorts, in the front of which she carried a small apron for checks and pens and pads of paper. Her hair was in pigtails.

The place was quiet given it was a weekday afternoon in downtown Long Beach. Saunders had let his second class go early in anticipation of spring break.

"So they removed the target," Adam said. "And when the dust settled they realized she had a bag full of groceries she was bringing to them."

They ordered a pitcher of beer and wings.

The waitress smiled and took the menus from them.

"Some guys," Adam said, "were told to carry extra weapons in case they accidentally shot a civilian so they could drop it on the body and make it look like they'd been attacked by an insurgent."

When the beer arrived, the waitress poured each glass slowly to avoid too much foam at the top.

"To Henry David Thoreau," Adam said, before sipping his

beer. "Even if he only went to jail for one night."

"You could go a lot longer," Saunders said.

He took a sip of his beer.

"One thing I've noticed," Saunders continued, "is most acts of civil disobedience have failed."

"Tell that to Martin Luther King," Adam said. "But I guess it depends how you view it. Do you want to be an object of history or an agent of history?"

When the wings came they were hot and steaming and messy looking. Saunders could smell the heat. The wings came in mild, medium, or *scorcher* and they had opted for *scorcher*. He grabbed one and bit into it. Not bad. His mouth and his lips were on fire. He wiped them with a napkin.

"1933," Adam said. "Germany. A widening gap between the government and the people. Sound familiar? Do you think this is a coincidence? Read any account of Nazi Germany and the signs were all there. It's a gradual shift. Things take place slowly. Crises, reforms, constant emergencies. All a charade to make the people constantly give allegiance. More and more bureaucracy and less government oversight. Meanwhile, nobody sees what's really happening beneath the surface. The process of anything democratic eroding way."

"We're a long way from Nazi Germany," Saunders said. "Don't you think that's just a bit extreme?"

"That's the point," Adam said. "Extreme times call for extreme measures. They want you to feel like a freak for thinking everything's a conspiracy. Look what they do to people who bring up these things—instant mockery. Even you!"

"Don't believe everything you read, Adam," Saunders said. "I used to be your age, too."

"It's got nothing to do with age, sir."

"The fact is nobody is in control," Saunders said. "It's all just chaos. Nobody knows what the fuck is going on."

"The people at the top do," Adam said. "The ones running the world. You think corporate power doesn't have a role in what's going on? The government's afraid of what will happen when the people find out what's going on behind the scenes. And the first thing they'll do is disarm us by taking away our guns."

Saunders's problem with all these conspiracy theories was not only that he'd outgrown them and saw them as the exclusive platform of the paranoid and the young, but that despite his resistance, there was always a morsel of truth to them. He didn't doubt that powerful institutions were in control of everything. He didn't doubt that all these wars, all these crises, though not an organized collusion, were in some unconscious way orchestrated by people in power to maintain that power. He didn't doubt Washington wasn't really all that concerned about the middle class or that he'd never earn an honest wage as an adjunct. But Adam's theories were all so vague. Shadowy types running the world. *What's really going on.* It was always the exclusive role of the conspiracy theorists to tell the rest of us *what's really going on.*

"I don't think there's a conspiracy to take away your guns if that's what you're saying," Saunders said.

"What do you mean when you say 'conspiracy' anyway?"

Adam said. "That's the first question. Why is someone a conspiracy theorist just because they don't believe the government account of something. Isn't that plain old skepticism?"

There didn't seem to be much difference between Democrat and Republican conspiracy theories, they just switched to whoever happened to be in power, but they always revolved around somebody lying. There also didn't seem to be much difference between Hooters and any other restaurant either—except the skimpier clothes.

The daytime crowd seemed normal, coming in for happy hour after work just as he and Adam were doing, in a sense. It was true, not exactly the kind of place you'd take your date, but as Saunders looked around the restaurant, the ratio between men and women seemed even. Everything was pleasant. Women sat around the tables, mostly office types, with their male co-workers, not necessarily drinking beer (though some of them were), but other cocktails. They ate chicken wings and stared up at the ten thousand televisions just like everybody else, not appearing stupid, or oppressed, or judgmental of the waitresses. Simply relieved to be out of the office for the day and, like the men, ready to enjoy themselves.

"The states have no rights anymore," Adam said. "The Feds are too big. They've taken control of everything."

"Let me ask you something," Saunders said. "Why'd you join the military then?"

Adam took a sip of his beer.

"Not a lot of other choices where I come from," he said. "And

I'm a patriot, I guess. But back then I only had a mythical perception of what war was like. When you're over there, all you can think about is your mission. You don't think about your country or even fighting for it. You fight for each other. But now I've had more time to think about it. I'm not naïve anymore. And yet, still, all I can think about is going back there."

"To the war?"

"Yes," Adam said.

"I thought you don't trust the government."

"I don't know how to explain it," Adam said, "but when you're over there, despite the terror of it, you don't have a self to face. There's no individual consciousness. In all truth, looking back, I probably joined to get away from myself for a while."

"What about your father?"

"My father had been gone a long time already."

"You never told me what happened," he said.

"It's not an easy story to tell," Adam said.

"For another time then," Saunders said, remembering Adam was still his student and he didn't want to pry.

Adam wasn't eating much. Saunders shoved another chicken wing in his mouth.

"No," Adam said. "It's all right. In the war it made us better soldiers to share with each other."

"We're not soldiers," Saunders said. "I'm your professor. But okay. Fair enough."

He took another sip of his beer that briefly left a foam mustache on his upper lip, which he wiped.

"It was suicide," Adam said. "He did it in the garage with the ignition running. He was a bad alcoholic. My mother found him."

"How old were you?"

"I was in my first year of high school," Adam said.

The steam was still coming off the wings, but everything was cooling down. Saunders didn't know what to say, so he just kept eating.

"What about you?" Adam said. "You never told me the whole story."

"Ah, well," Saunders said. He'd forgotten about his own little lie. He stopped chewing on the meat in his mouth and swallowed it. "Let's get back to saving the country."

All that was left on Saunders's plate was a pile of bones.

"There was an explosion," Saunders said.

"What kind of an explosion?" Adam asked.

"The guy in the office above him," Saunders said.

"What about him?"

He pushed his plate aside, feeling guilty about the meat he was going to have to add to the bones of his little lie.

"Some kind of chemist or rocket scientist," Saunders said. "You know how those guys are. Mixing the wrong chemicals. Blew up his own office and the lower half of the building caught fire."

"Holy shit," Adam said. "What kind of chemicals? What do you mean? Why was he doing this in an office in the first place?"

"Nobody knows."

Saunders himself wouldn't have believed this story if it hadn't been somewhat based on an article he had read about Jack Parsons

—a famous rocket scientist, religious wacko, and friend of Aleister Crowley—who had died this way.

"Some of the details are still real fuzzy of how that happened. My mother's never really explained it to me."

"That's insane," Adam said.

Sometimes it haunted him to think his father might still be out there somewhere. Other times, it haunted him even more to think that maybe he was dead.

"Yeah," Saunders said. "It was pretty haunting."

"At least you can say it was an accident," Adam said. "It took years for me to understand my father suffered from mental illness. I think he had been self-medicating all those years with alcohol. It haunts me to think I could've done something."

Their pitcher was almost empty and the thought of going home made Saunders feel lonely.

"I guess that's why you gotta make something of your life while you still can," Adam said.

"You have a real talent for words, Adam," Saunders said. "There's a scholarship in the English Department and I think you should apply."

He explained the details of it, how there'd be no other requirement than for him to submit the essay he'd already written.

"What do you think?" he asked.

Adam took the last sip of his beer then said, "I don't really see the point."

"The point is a thousand dollars," Saunders said.

"I know all about words," Adam said. "How many times have

you gotten what you wanted by writing something? The truth is the world doesn't care about words. There are too many of them as it is. Too many essays. Too many poems. Too many novels. Too much talk on the radio, the news, the classroom. It's not enough. It never changes anything."

"Well, think about it," Saunders said.

The bill came and Adam threw down the cash for his portion, then slid out of the booth, ready to leave.

"Where you going?" Saunders asked. "It's spring break."

"I have plans to make," Adam said.

"You could die," Saunders said.

"I accept that," Adam said. "That's something you learn in the rush of war. How to accept your own destruction."

After he left, Saunders stayed and ordered another pitcher. The afternoon sun had been covered up by the marine layer like it always was this time of year, already reminding him of the June gloom that would cover the whole city in a couple of months. Something he might not get to see this year or ever again.

He was drunk already and it wasn't even dark out. Maybe he'd be brave enough to go somewhere and meet a woman. Or maybe once he digested those chicken wings, he'd be nothing but chicken shit. Chickens were nasty little frightful creatures, weren't they? Like rabbits. Nothing but dumb. He didn't feel an ounce of guilt eating them.

It probably wasn't the best idea to do anything but go home. When the waitress delivered his pitcher, he realized if he wasn't already wasted, he'd definitely be by the time he finished this beer. The restaurant had begun to fill up with more happy hour patrons when Saunders looked over at the bar and saw the back of a familiar head. He picked up his newly poured pitcher, his glass, and headed over to it.

"Ray," he said.

Zapata turned to look at him and nodded.

Saunders took the stool next to him.

"Did I tell about this tree I got in my backyard?" Ray said.

Saunders shook his head no and took a sip of his beer.

"It's this old Monterrey Pine," Ray said, "and it's been getting too close to my roof. Well, anyway, people keep telling me to cut the thing down and all this bullshit and I keep telling them no way. Then it hit me: don't cut the tree, cut the house."

CHAPTER 30

Taking a Position

This massacre seemed to be going on longer than Saunders had imagined. Especially having seen so many news reports of mass shootings over the years. What this moment needed was a good editor. It was true, as of late, he tended to get more bored than usual. But how long could this go on? It could be hours, days, holed up on the classroom floor.

Lying here, in this position, reminded him of the time Kathy dragged them to Bikram Yoga.

"You might like it," she joked. "The guy who started it's a real asshole."

It had been a good time in their relationship; early enough to still feel excited over love, when they could retain a sense of humor before sensitivities got too much in the way, but late enough that they were comfortable together. That great middle period in the lives of a couple, in which they actually could live life comfortably without the jangling nerves of getting to know each other or the boiling blood of getting to un-know each other.

He had found himself in a crowded sauna, drenched in his own sweat, trying to make his body do things it had never done before. For a man in his late thirties, the instructor joked afterwards, he had the flexibility of a fifty-seven-year-old.

"My treat," Kathy had said when she'd first suggested it, knowing he couldn't afford to go to yoga every week. Ever since she'd gotten her full-time job, she made twice as much and taught half as many classes.

About thirty men and women spread out on mats across a grimy floor in a 105-degree room. Exchange the mats for desks and it was his classroom on the hotter days of the semester. It smelled like it, too. When he first walked into the studio, he couldn't help but gag at the dense fart stench that seemed to inhabit every inch of the room.

"It's all mind control," Kathy told him, reading a pamphlet given to them. "It's a battle of the will!"

He read the first page of the pamphlet called *The Five Aspects of Mind*, which were Faith, Self-Control, Determination, Concentration, and Patience.

What makes your soul happy? This was written at the top.

A cigarette. A cigarette would make my soul happy.

Kathy had ordered yoga mats for both of them online, but they hadn't arrived in time, so the instructor found them two used mats for the day, and Saunders couldn't help but imagine the vials of other people's sweat seeping into them. *Doesn't this violate some kind of health code?* He was repulsed at the idea of spending the next ninety minutes on some yoga mat that who knew what kind of sick or diseased person had emitted all their toxins into. Kathy had already gotten down on her knees and into some stretching position.

"We have to take the first position," Kathy said. "You ready?"

"Let's do this," he said, clapping his hands together.

The Five Aspects of Lying: Faith, Self-Control, Determination,

Concentration, Patience.

He took the position. Kathy placed the pamphlet on the floor in front of them. Bikram Yoga had twenty-six postures. All of which they would be doing in the next ninety minutes. And all written in Sanskrit.

Some people gave up and just sat on the mat unable to do anything else. A couple times, he had been sweaty enough and exhausted enough to want to walk out the door himself, except he was too exhausted to walk at all. He didn't think the place could stink worse than when he came in, but it did. Everyone's sweat mingling together in the atmosphere, raising the temperature, and creating a humidity of bad sweat to breathe in.

"This has to be unhealthy," he whispered to Kathy.

"It's good for you," she said.

But it was only the last, and arguably, most important posture that would be any good for him. In Sanskrit, they called it *savasana*. In regular old English, it was known as "corpse pose."

CHAPTER 31
Club Book

"I just loved how Cervantes used metafictionality to draw attention to the fictionality," Kelley Glazer said.

Leave it to the Glazers to have scheduled the next book club meeting during spring break.

"What's the name of the club again, Teacher?" Liz joked, when Saunders had picked her up that evening. She did look dressed for it though with a short black dress, leather jacket, and high-heeled boots.

The first thing Saunders had noticed before knocking on Glazers' door was the giant wooden Easter Bunny on the front lawn. Sure, it was less than a week away from the holiday, but as far as he knew, the Glazers didn't have any children, or at least he hadn't ever noticed any. After Saunders and Liz were welcomed inside, Liz's boots clicked across the entryway.

"I think it really plays with the question of the reliability and *reality* of the text," Paul Cross said. "Also, a tremendous mix of the sacred and the profane. Probably the first postmodern novel. Almost like he becomes the text itself."

"I found it to be just a little phallogocentric for my taste," said the super-sized hunchback whose name Saunders had finally learned was Cheryl.

"What I really enjoyed," Bill Gandy said, "is the way Cervantes plays with this notion of hyperreality."

"I think it's about hope," Saunders said. "The hope of shaping one's existence. The hope of making the fantasy world real."

There was silence after his comment, which had come to be the norm. For a minute, everyone looked at each other, as if trying to decipher if there was a deeper theoretical meaning hidden behind his statement.

"Teacher," Liz whispered, "you weren't kidding that everyone here would be white."

They sat on a beanbag in Glazers' living room, having shown up too late to get a seat on either of the two couches or half dozen chairs put out.

"Well, that's a pretty ironic hope," Bill Gandy said, with a smirk. "I mean, if Don Quixote is the text itself, what can we make of the end?"

"All narratives are futile, meaningless, unstable...fantasy?" George said.

Saunders hadn't made it to the end yet. He was still adrift in the adventure of the narrative. Maybe he wanted to stop time for a little while longer, savor it. Everything had a daze over it these last few weeks; it seemed as if he was racing to the finish line, or the *finished* line. Things were moving much quicker than even he'd anticipated.

"I see it as just the opposite of hope," Bill Gandy carried on. "I see it as deconstructing the poetry and chivalric romance on the post-pastiche spatiality and re-organizing and representing their instability with complete hyper-contemporaneity."

"Teacher," Liz whispered into Saunders's ear, "I liked your

idea about hope, but I don't really get what most of these people are talking about."

"Don't worry," Saunders said, "they don't either."

"Also, my leg's asleep," Liz said.

She shifted her body on the beanbag and Saunders scooted over a bit more to give her room.

"And, of course," George said, "even Sancho Panza, the one who seems to believe the most in his master, right from the beginning of the second half, essentially acknowledges his master is insane. At the very least he wants a salary." George opened his book. "Look at Chapter VII, page 499."

Everyone, including Saunders, who'd managed to set his copy of the book down between his legs while he sipped his sangria, opened up to the page. Liz moved in closer, squinting her eyes and holding onto the book for both of them to read.

"'Remember Sancho, that fine hopes are better than miserable possessions.' I love that line," George said. "Reminds me of what Berlin's saying. So, let me ask you guys...does Don Quixote have 'fine hopes'?"

"I wouldn't call them 'fine'," said Jim Rice, with a face that looked to be in permanent distress, like he just had a tooth pulled. Apparently, they had met at the first book club, but Saunders couldn't remember. "He just wants fame, doesn't he? As he tells Sancho shortly after that: people value fame even if it's negative. And, of course, he has to give it up in the end."

"Which is interesting, of course, if you think about that line—today it still rings true," Cheryl said.

"I love that part," George said, keeping his book open, "when Quixote tells Sancho that the world already has enough saints, what it needs is for him to be an errant knight."

"Sure, but to break that down even further, he already is the book itself. So again, we have almost simulacra upon simulacra upon simulacra."

"Isn't that redundant?" Paul Cross said.

Everybody laughed, some harder than they needed to, just to show they got the joke.

"Of course," George said, "everything changes in the end. What did you guys think? Is this book a tragedy? A comedy? I mean, we know Gatsby ends up dead in the pool, and Ahab sinks the ship and kills everyone, but what about Quixote?"

"I think he comes to his right mind," Kelley said. "And finally accepts reality. You can't just go on living a hyper-real existence all the time."

"I read an interesting essay about the novel," George said. "It was a feminist interpretation of his desire to control his niece by telling her what kind of man she can and can't marry. Anyway, the really interesting part is the kind of man he tells her she can't marry is a man who knows 'anything about books and chivalry'."

"If that were my uncle, I'd tell him to go stuff it," Cheryl said.

Everybody laughed again.

Liz raised her hand.

"I thought the end was really sad," she said to Saunders's astonishment, his not having any clue she'd ever read the book.

"Of course, Teacher," she whispered to him when he mentioned it, "not only teachers read books you know."

"That's exactly right," George said. "The book is sad. After all, what does he have left? Everyone else in the book goes back to their families. Even Sancho. The only women in Quixote's life are his niece and housekeeper. Other than that, he's alone and has to renounce his love for Dulcinea, knowing she's merely a figment of his imagination. What is sadder than knowing the love of your life is only in your head? And how many of us have done this? I know I've had my share of delusion when it comes to love."

Kelley put her hands on her hips.

"When I was younger, honey," he said to her. "Not now, of course."

"Yeah, poor Quixote," Roseanna Young said, who wasn't young at all, but old and humorless, in slacks and a turtleneck sweater. "After all, he only has two women to pamper him and look after him and that he can boss around all the time. And the princess is just a figment of his imagination."

"A man needs a woman to take care of him or he falls apart," said Liz. "The same is true of a woman needing a man. Quixote's lucky in that he has his housekeeper and niece, but he's missing a great love in his life."

"You're hot when you talk about books," Saunders whispered in her ear. Liz giggled from his tickling breath and put her hand over her ear.

"Teacher," she said, "I think you're getting more drunk than everyone else."

He grabbed her waist and pulled her closer to him.

"Oh yes," Roseanna said, sarcastically, breaking the silence caused by everyone staring at them. "Don Quixote is all about what he lacks. After all, in the end, he is a knight who has no one to save. He needs his damsel in distress."

"And don't forget the donkey," Bill Gandy said. "We haven't talked about the donkey."

"And how once he renounces everything he ceases to exist," Paul Cross said.

"If I have to sit here one minute longer, I'm going to cease to exist," Saunders whispered in Liz's ear.

"Teacher," Liz said, putting her hand on his knee, "stop it!"

"Why don't you be a good teacher's pet and go make out with me in the bathroom," Saunders whispered to Liz.

"No, Teacher, no," she whispered back. "Control yourself."

"Are we supposed to feel sorry for this lunatic?" said Maureen Freeman, a colleague of Kelley's. "I mean, the only part I liked in the whole book was the end."

"I don't know," Liz said, trying to comport herself and jump back into the conversation. "I generally prefer a happy ending."

"The only thing happy about this ending is that he stops being crazy."

"You don't feel sorry for people who are crazy?" Liz said. "They suffer more."

"I didn't say I don't feel sorry for people who are crazy," Maureen said. "I just said it's good that he stops being one of them."

Saunders leaned over and whispered in Liz's ear, "You get an 'A' for the semester."

She blushed.

"Stop flattering me, Teacher," she said.

"Well," George said, interrupting, "if you consider dying the solution to stopping 'being crazy.' I guess the question is, at this point, is it better to die with the illusion of himself as a knight errant? Does it make any difference if he dies aware of the stark reality of the world and the fleeting fantasy of his own imagination?"

"Whether we like it or not," Roseanna Young said, "there is an objective reality. Is it better to die in delusion? Are you saying that it's better for someone to die believing in heaven than, say, seeing the world for what it is?"

"It'd certainly make the journey easier," Bill Gandy said. "But what would it mean about the rest of your life? What kind of life aren't you leading if you go around believing that after you die is when life really begins?"

"I believe in heaven, Teacher," Liz whispered in Saunders's ear. "Is that dumb?"

"The point is, I think," George said, always the rational moderator, "that no matter what we do, somehow we're living under some kind of delusion. Like the greatest delusion of all, of course, that we aren't going to die."

"So why not make it grand?" Saunders said. "Wasn't this the beauty of the book? What's great about this book is the way it plays with what is real and what is fantasy."

"Good answer, Teacher," Liz said.

Just then Kelley, who Saunders hadn't noticed get up from the conversation, came back from the kitchen ringing an old-fashioned bell and said,

"Ding, ding, ding, dinnertime."

Everybody stood up at once as if already tired of the conversation, and headed to the table in the dining room where Kelley had made a beautiful spread that included a variety of foods: plates of cheeses, two salads, sausages, and cornbread. There were also desserts: cupcakes, tiramisu, and cookies that people had brought, all to be swashed down with six bottles of two buck Chuck.

"Teacher," Liz said. "You didn't tell me it was a pot luck. We should have stopped and bought something."

"Don't be silly," he said, "and you didn't tell me you had read the book."

"I didn't, Teacher," she said. "I lied."

He clicked his plastic cup, filled with what was left of the sangria, against hers.

"Let's get out of here," he said.

"Shouldn't we say goodbye first?" Liz said.

"I'll email George tomorrow."

He was turned on. He grabbed Liz's hand and they slipped away from the crowd in the kitchen and out through the front door, almost knocking down the wooden Easter Bunny on their way out.

CHAPTER 32

Attendance Is Mandatory

That Sunday, Saunders drove out to Hemet to see his mother for Easter. He hated the desert and couldn't understand why in the hell old people and hipsters liked it so much. His mother claimed she liked the heat and the proximity to all the Indian casinos. She had sold his grandparents' house, her inheritance, a few years back when she got a good deal from a friend's daughter, a real estate agent, who convinced her to buy a smaller one-story two-bedroom house in a planned over-55 retirement community called "The Four Seasons."

At least it kept him from worrying about her. And there were things to do: water aerobics, golf, yoga, movies, and a clubhouse with a cafeteria where she could share communal meals and make friends with other residents. These over-55 planned communities of the twenty-first century were now full of the same people who invested their youth in the communes of free love and peace during the sixties and seventies—except now they played golf instead of acoustic guitar and took different kinds of drugs. Mostly, they were widowers or soon to be ones. Except his mother, of course, who had never married. Only once had he even known her to date anyone. He had been very young the last (and only) time his mother introduced him to someone even remotely close to a boyfriend—a man named Gary, who the seven-year-old Saunders secretly believed might be his father, and even when he had doubts, wanted it to be true so badly that whenever Gary came over, he clung to him. For years, he feared he was responsible for the breakup between Gary and his mother. He wanted Gary to like him so much that, one night, as a gift, he gave him a dried squid he got the year before at Sea World. It was a strange present, for sure, and maybe he shouldn't have been so surprised when he found it at the bottom of the trashcan. But soon after Gary stopped returning his mother's phone calls. His mother never brought another man around him after that.

The day of his visit was a warm spring afternoon and the moderate Southern California version of winter had already thawed. Saunders stopped off at a See's Candy on the way over and bought a chocolate egg on clearance. There had been times in the past few years when he hadn't even bothered seeing his mother at Easter. It was a holiday that seemed to be slowly fading from the American psyche and he wondered if there just wasn't enough market value in it. Unlike some of the other big holidays, obviously Christmas, but also Thanksgiving, which had essentially begun to get marketed as the night before Black Friday, Easter had little connection to buying stuff. It was on the unserious level of Halloween now.

For him, Easter usually meant the end of spring break. It amazed him to think that at almost forty-years-old, he still had a spring break even though most of the time, split between two different community colleges, it rarely added up to a full week off, but rather two half-weeks. But this year was different. The college planets had aligned.

He hadn't seen his mother since Christmas and with his

recent depression had even slipped up on making regular phone calls. Maybe it was some pending guilt about facing her mother, knowing the plot boiling inside of him. Would this be the last time he saw her?

Saunders was greeted at the door by Rita, his mother's long-time roommate. She had white hair and thick glasses and was probably in her mid-seventies, a bit older than his mother, who had just turned 70.

"Hi sweetie," Rita said, opening the door wider for him to enter.

His mother was trying to hang a reproduction she had recently bought of a Robert Doisneau photograph of five female hairstylists basking in the sun at a Paris café. It made him think of Adam's paper. *We were a long way off from Paris.*

A long way off.

The television was playing one of the *I Love Lucy* DVDs Saunders bought his mother for Christmas.

She looked as if she'd aged five years since he'd last seen her. She had stopped dyeing her hair and had recently cut it short. Each time he saw her, she seemed to have shrunken more. The weight gained at midlife nearly gone now, and with her hair short and gray, and her oversized pink sweatshirt that said "Pechanga" on it in gold sequins, she looked like the friendly neighbor who might bring you cookies during the holidays.

"My favorite son," she said, looking over at Rita, and then giving him a kiss.

"Your only son, Lyn," Rita said.

"Your only child," Saunders said. "At least that Rita and I know of."

They all laughed.

"Here," his mother said, dragging him over to the kitchen table and handing him a Starbucks gift card. "I figured you were too old for a bunny."

He handed her the egg.

"How's everything?" Saunders asked.

"Hey," his mother said, "come out in the garage. I wanna show you something."

He followed her out.

"Look," she said, pointing to a golf cart parked next to her car. "Isn't it neat? Rita just bought it. We use it all the time now to get around the community. Wanna give it a ride? We could take it to the clubhouse for lunch."

"Maybe later," Saunders said. His mother had taken him and Kathy to the clubhouse cafeteria for lunch once before and he promised himself he would never make that mistake again. The food had been bland and all the seniors had depressed him. Not to mention there wasn't a bar.

When they returned from the garage, Rita disappeared into her room and it was just the two of them.

"So what's new?" he asked, raiding his mother's fridge like a teenager, disappointed she didn't have any beer, but settling on a Coke.

"We went to church this morning," his mother said. "That was new."

It certainly was. He'd never heard his mother mention church before, but he supposed she was getting to that age. He had never been a believer; in fact, he hated religion. But for a moment, maybe for the first time in his adult life, Saunders found himself thinking about the story of Jesus and the idea of being a martyr; upon his death, what would he be a martyr for? Had he not felt on the cross lately? A martyr for nothing on a cross that symbolized nothing.

He sat down on his mother's white couch. She loved buying everything in white. After moving out from his grandparents' sometime during middle school, their first apartment had been all white. White couch, white coffee table, white curtains, white carpet. White television. It'd been so long since he'd had a television he couldn't help but stare at it. He knew almost every episode of *I Love Lucy*, having watched it his whole life. These were the later episodes. The ones with little Ricky.

"She's just so racist and submissive," Kathy once said of Lucy.

But as a kid, he was fascinated by 1950s television and the idea of his mother and father living as a family in the same house together. Every semester he made his students deconstruct a Norman Rockwell painting of a Thanksgiving dinner with a happy 1940s family sitting around a dining room table, everybody smiling. This always got laughs. The painting was called *Freedom from Want* and despite his classroom analysis of the painting, Saunders had always kind of liked it. A fantasy that still appealed to him no matter how false the image was.

"What if grandma didn't *want* to be in the kitchen all day?" he asked his class. "What if grandma *wanted* to be a lawyer?"

Some of his students would nod their heads. Most of his life, he didn't have to worry too much about the reinforcement of traditional gender roles as there had only ever been him and his mother and neither one of them liked turkey. What would it have been like to have a mother in the kitchen? A father to carve the turkey? Two sets of grandparents?

"Whatever happened to that guy Gary?" Saunders asked, setting his Coke can down on the white coffee table and leaning back into the couch.

"Who?" his mother said, as if merely a reflex reaction to hearing a name long forgotten in the past.

"Gary," he said. "You know, that guy you used to date?"

It took some coaching for her to remember, but then she did.

"Oh yes, *that* Gary," his mother said. "Who knows? He's probably dead." It might have been shocking if not for his mother's age and the fact that she lived in a retirement community where a new widow was made every minute. Plus, it was probably the truth, statistically anyway, male life spans being what they were. That was a problem he'd avoid by dying young. He'd never make a widow of any woman.

"I used to think he was my father," Saunders said.

"Does it make you sad?" his mother asked.

"Not really," he said. "Sometimes, I think it's possible my real dad could be dead too."

"I'm sorry, Berlin," his mother said.

That name. Most of his childhood he had hated it. His mother, whose full name was Marilyn, liked that the ends of their first names had the same sound.

"What can I say? I was a hippie," she once told him when he asked her about it. "I wanted something different. Something hopeful. Not to mention it was going to be perfect whether you ended up a boy or a girl."

"You named me after a city divided by a wall," he'd said. "And that was supposed to be hopeful?"

"And look what happened?" she said. "That wall came down."

Eventually he had come to love the originality of her choice to name him after a city. It had only recently become trendy to name children after cities like Paris or London, both of which he was relieved she hadn't picked for him. He supposed if he had to be named after a city, better Berlin, than say, Detroit. Detroit Saunders. Although it did have a nice ring to it—for a weatherman. Or a porn star.

"I was thinking," his mother said, sitting down on the couch beside him, "that you could stay the night."

She was always trying to get him to stay longer and he was always trying to do the bare minimum, something that also made him feel guilty. This year was even harder. Without a woman in his life, the thought of staying at his mother's seemed all the more depressing. At least when Kathy was around, it didn't seem so pathetic. Luckily, his mother hadn't asked him anything about her. He'd had to explain to her at Christmas why Kathy wasn't with him and now it was like she'd never existed.

"I wish I could stay," Saunders said, "but tomorrow's Monday." He failed to mention he'd already been off all week.

"How's school anyway?" his mother asked.

"School's fine," he said.

"My son, the college student. I'm so proud of you," his mother said. "What classes are you taking?"

"None, Mom," Saunders said. "I'm a teacher, remember?"

He wasn't sure if he should feel offended or worried that she didn't remember what he did for a living. Was it the first sign of Alzheimer's? Dementia? Or just the product of old age? But she wasn't *that* old. Suddenly he felt really guilty about leaving her alone in this world. With any luck, maybe she'd forget him, too.

"Oh, that's right," his mother said. "What subject again?"

"English."

"Oh, English," his mother said, staring off at the TV as if some faint image of the past had just come across it. "English was my favorite subject."

CHAPTER 33

Proffesional Development

On his way home from the desert, Saunders stopped off at Starbucks to use his gift card. He avoided going to the one by campus because, Easter Sunday or not, it was inevitable he'd run into a colleague—though none would openly admit to getting their coffee from a corporate café. Even more offensive was that the name was stolen from a character in *Moby Dick* though nobody cared, remembered, or even knew that. Starbucks was just a place for bourgeois people to order small, medium, and large in Italian.

On the occasion that he did go, he saw fellow adjuncts sitting with their laptops, working on lesson plans in between the classes they held at different schools, and without any actual office. He'd never really known what a lesson plan was. "How many preps?" one of his colleagues asked him one semester when he'd taken on an extra class at a third school. He'd never thought to ask anyone such a question, and wasn't even really sure what a "prep" was. Did it mean the five minutes of reviewing a story or article before class or sometimes *in* class? Hadn't he been prepping his whole life? When he taught, all the knowledge he'd ever known came out in one form or another, as did all the neuroses, all the defensiveness, all the tragic and happy moments. There wasn't really any way to "prep" that.

The line was long and Saunders ended up being the guy in the awkward position of waiting while simultaneously holding open the door for those entering and exiting.

"Tall non-fat latte with carmel drizzle…"

"Tall, half-caff soy latte at 120 degrees…"

"Venti, half and half, 10 pumps vanilla, extra whip…"

What Starbucks stopped serving was anything resembling coffee. No wonder students expected A's on all their essays. Starbucks gave you whatever you wanted and did it with a smile. Amazing how the employees could repeat everything just heard. It took swift cognitive skills to even work at this place. Good thing the employees stayed amped up on free caffeine all day. Maybe working at Starbucks wasn't much different than teaching—each customer having their own individual demands and expectations, not to mention having to learn everybody's names. He'd always hated how they asked for your name. Not to be bothered, he would lie and say his name was Ben. Even after simplifying his name though, he often wound up with "Bin" on his cup.

"Venti Iced Skinny Hazelnut Macchiato, Sugar-Free syrup, Extra Shot, Light Ice, No Whip…"

It was his turn.

"Americano," he said.

"Size?" the cashier asked.

"Medium," he said.

"Grande Americano," she shouted to the barista. He handed her his gift card and she swiped it.

"I'm sorry," she said. "It doesn't seem to be going through."

"I've never used it," he said. "Can you try again?"

She swiped again.

"Says your balance is zero."

His mother had re-gifted him a used gift card. He pulled out his debit card.

After he paid, he walked over to the pickup counter to wait for his Americano when out of the corner of his eye he saw a man emerge from the back room, tying a green apron around his waist. A familiar face peeked out of a black hat. It was Tom Corona. What was he doing there? Tom had never mentioned working at Starbucks before. The whole thing was disorienting. What did it mean? Without seeing Saunders, Tom rushed up to help the other barista, his head down, emptying the espresso in a measuring cup. A huge line of cups awaited him and his coworker. He looked so small and pathetic with his green apron as he repeated the cashier's next order, "Non-Fat Frappuccino with Extra Whipped Cream and Chocolate Sauce."

Meanwhile, Saunders lingered behind the large crowd that had formed, all waiting impatiently for their drinks, most looking down at their phones, pacing back and forth, or taking a seat on one of the green stools by the window.

"Excuse me," said a pink-faced woman with frizzy blonde hair. "How much longer is it going to take?"

Tom looked up at her and smiled.

"I apologize," he said. "What was it you ordered, ma'am?"

The woman sighed and looked at the other customers and rolled her eyes.

"Mine was the grande extra shot soy with extra foam, split with a half squirt of sugar-free vanilla and a half squirt of sugar-free cinnamon, a half packet of Splenda, and extra whipped cream."

Tom looked at her and kept his smile.

"You mean half-*pump*, not *squirt*. Coming right up," he said, turning around to grab the whipped cream from the refrigerator.

Other customers began to get antsy. A guy in a suit, probably coming from Easter mass, walked up to the bar and slid his cup back over to Tom.

"This was supposed to be iced."

Two more people complained because their cups were too hot and he had forgotten to give them the sleeve protector for their fragile hands.

Meanwhile, the drink orders kept coming and Tom and his co-worker, student-age, maybe just barely twenty, kept repeating them.

"Can you make sure that's 160 degrees?" said a lesbian in a t-shirt and jeans, with a faux hawk, leaning over the counter to get Tom's attention.

Saunders watched him wipe the perspiration off his bald head and felt sorry for him.

"You'd think they'd have more help," an older man with a dyed beard complained to another man. "This is ridiculous. How long have you been waiting?"

The customer he complained to looked at his phone.

"At least five minutes," the other man said.

And Saunders thought students were demanding?

Tom's apron was covered in espresso as he rushed to make drinks, constantly bending down to get milk out of the refrigerator.

"Do you have a straw?" another woman said.

Saunders listened as the long line of names were called out one by one. Tom hadn't seen him standing there. He felt the compassionate impulse to slip out and not let Tom see him at all, but he wanted his drink.

When it was his turn, Tom looked at the cup kind of funny, and then called out his name. Saunders approached the counter. Tom, disoriented at first, did a double-take and then his face turned beet red.

"Berlin," he said.

"Hi, Tom," Saunders said, noticing this time they'd written his name as *Been*.

"Christ," Tom said. "I had no choice. Without that other class, it was either this or sleep in my car."

Cups were lined up behind him, but Tom was frozen. Every semester, for twelve years, Saunders had feared a similar fate. He'd heard horror stories of classes being taken from adjuncts at the last minute and given to full-timers, but he had somehow narrowly escaped this.

"Please," Tom said, "don't tell anyone you saw me here."

The other customers were getting antsy with Tom and the cashier was calling out his name.

"Seriously," Tom said, before returning to the line of cups backed up for him. "I'll do anything."

"Don't worry," Saunders said, grabbing his drink before walking away, knowing exactly what *anything* was going to be.

CHAPTER 34

ADDITIONAL MATERIALS

From: Berlin Saunders
To: Tom Corona
Subject: Scholarship

Hello Tom,

Good seeing you tonight, and I completely understand where you're coming from. Isn't the adjunct life great? I've attached a Word document of the essay I told you about for the scholarship. The student has been very reluctant about applying so let's keep it a secret. I've included his ID number below. Let me know if you need anything else.

Best,

Berlin

ID number: 0001596853

Adamsessay1.docx

From: Tom Corona

To: Berlin Saunders

Subject: Re: Scholarship

Got it. Good seeing you too. And thanks for understanding. Fingers crossed for the WAC job.

Tom

CHAPTER 35

Coarse Evaluation

"'"The white moderate who is more devoted to 'order' than to justice; who prefers a negative peace which is the absence of tension to a positive peace which is the presence of justice; who constantly says I agree with you in the goal you seek, but I can't agree with your methods of direct action...'"'

Adam looked up from the book and stopped reading the passage.

"So, who is King referring to when he says 'white moderate'?" Saunders asked the class.

Romeo Flores raised his hand.

"White people?" he said.

"White people, yes," Saunders said. "But what does he mean more specifically?"

"Racist white people?" Justin Keneficke piped in.

"He's specifically talking about the eight white Alabama clergymen," Beverly MacDowell said. "Who he's addressing in this letter."

Adam nodded his head in agreement. "The ones who don't think it's the right time to take any action."

"But what does he mean by 'moderate'? And what does he say is the 'white moderate's' failure'?" Saunders said.

"They want the process of integration to be handled in the courts," Beverly said.

"He's pointing out their hypocrisy," Adam said. "Their failure is they claim to support his cause, but on the other hand are more 'devoted to order than to justice.'"

"And what's wrong with that, according to King?"

"He says right here," Beverly said, pointing to a passage in her book. "'Shallow understanding from people of good will is more frustrating than absolute misunderstanding from people of ill will. Lukewarm acceptance is much more bewildering than outright rejection.'"

"In other words," Adam said, "they're not really on his side. They're only pretending. They don't care if injustice prevails as long as they can continue on with their safe blameless lives."

Saunders saw Beverly nod her head in agreement. To think, only weeks ago they were disagreeing about gun control. Now they were allies. These were the times he still felt his job rewarding. If a white, gun-toting young male could find common ground with a middle-aged black mother on the meaning of a text, maybe there was hope for this country.

"Let's back up a little," Saunders said, holding his book up in front of him. "Before his discussion of the white moderate. What are the four basic steps of non-violent direct action?"

"'Collection of facts, negotiation, self-purification, direct action,'" Adam read.

"Direct action comes last," Saunders said. "After every other possibility is exhausted."

"And it is," Adam said. "Which is the purpose of this letter. To explain that the cup of endurance has run dry and men need to take action."

"But only after attempts to negotiate have been made," Saunders said.

"Isn't negotiation the point of taking action?" Beverly asked.

"As he says," Adam said, "'Nonviolent direct action seeks to create such a crisis and establish such creative tension that a community that has constantly refused to negotiate is forced to confront the issue.'"

As Saunders had walked from the parking lot to his first class that morning, he'd felt a bigger sense of purpose than he had for a long time. Almost as if life were livable again. At first, he'd questioned the ethics of sending Adam's essay to Tom Corona without his consent, and even correcting a few typos here and there in the original draft, but now he felt good about his choice. He had taken action, hadn't he? He was on Adam's side, wasn't he? Adam refused to negotiate and he had forced him to confront the issue. It was an act of civil disobedience on Saunders's part. Surely, Adam would have to respect that. Besides, his winning the scholarship would make him feel more confident and might even convince him words were more powerful than trying to steal an American icon.

But the universe always had its way of humbling his good feelings and this time wasn't any different when in walked Harry Crawford carrying a yellow legal pad. It was just like Crawford to choose the first class after spring break to observe him, when both he and his students were still trying to adjust from vacation. But this time, Saunders didn't care. He felt good about the direction the class was going. Crawford's presence didn't feel threatening. He wasn't a monster today; he was a windmill.

Crawford nodded, waved his hand as if in apology for interrupting, and took an empty seat at the back of the class.

"Okay," Saunders said, as if the concentration of the class had not been broken, "next question: how does MLK feel about being labeled an extremist?"

"He doesn't mind it," Adam said.

"Can you think of any examples of 'extremists' that he gives us?"

Some of his students nodded their heads.

Tess Mackenzie's hand went up.

"Jesus," she said.

"Lincoln," Beverly said.

"Osama Bin Laden," Justin Keneficke said, making the class laugh.

"Jefferson," Adam said.

"Jefferson, of course, one of the great founding fathers whose ideology of equality was revolutionary at the time," Saunders said.

"He also sold his own children into slavery," interrupted Crawford, talking to the students around his desk.

"The point is," Saunders said, annoyed by Crawford's interruption, "the word extremism often gets associated with something negative these days, but here is King associating it with something more positive: an extremism for love. A different way of thinking about the word compared to what we hear today. One might be labeled an extremist, but an extremist in disobeying an unjust law. Which is what again?"

"Segregation," Nancy Choi said.

"Yes," Saunders said, "but more generally? If a 'just' law, according to King, is one that 'uplifts human personality,' then what is an 'unjust' law?"

"Don't do anything special," Crawford had told him when he'd run into him earlier in the semester. How long would he stay? Saunders looked at the clock. There were still ten minutes left to the class. He felt his left eye beginning to twitch.

"Anybody?"

"An unjust law," Crawford interrupted, "is a law that degrades human personality and one is morally obligated to disobey."

Anybody who is not the brooch-wearing chair of the fucking English Department?

Crawford scribbled something else down on his yellow legal pad after giving his answer. Saunders wanted to throw his dry erase marker at him.

"Can anyone think of a present law they might feel morally obligated to disobey?"

Vanessa Rivas, of course, was the only one to raise her hand. He tried his best to ignore her. He looked at Beverly and Adam to save him, but nobody took the bait. He looked at Crawford who avoided making eye contact with him and then back over to Vanessa. She looked pretty today. He'd give her that much. He could see her young bare legs showing slightly beneath her desk.

"Okay, Vanessa," he said, smiling nervously. "What do you got for us?"

She looked at him, surprised that after being ignored for so long the professor was calling on her.

"Well," she said, "it doesn't really have anything to do with the question."

This better be good. After all, if it was unavoidable, might as well make it fun. He watched as Crawford continued to scribble on his yellow notepad.

"What does it have to do with?"

Vanessa Rivas looked around the room, for once a little self-consciously.

"Your zipper's down," she said.

CHAPTER 36

SECONDARY SOURCES

Later that week, Saunders met up with Will who was back in town to do a one-off gig to promote his new album with the big nineties band.

"I'm so exhausted," Will said. "We were on Stern yesterday at six in the morning and then had to catch a flight here."

Reluctantly, he'd driven to pick Will up at his hotel in Hollywood and Will suggested they go to the classic landmark Musso & Frank nearby. Saunders had always wanted to eat there, but couldn't really afford it. Inside, with its art deco booths and art deco waiters in red jackets and bowties, you could pretend you were there with Faulkner, or John Fante, or F. Scott Fitzgerald.

It'd been at least a few years since he'd seen Will. In person, anyway. Saunders had seen him on YouTube clips and television shows, of course. But Will looked the same as he always did: skinny. Maybe a little older. But no glowing signs of his newfound impending rock stardom except the Ray-Bans he sported while waiting in front of the hotel for Saunders to pick him up, and the absence of his regular glasses since he'd been able to afford laser surgery.

"Check this out," Will said, showing him a picture he'd been sent of a beautiful Korean girl somewhere on the streets of Hollywood. "She says I'm her favorite guitar player."

"She's gorgeous," Saunders said.

We have rock star professions, Phil had said. It was one thing to have a rock star "profession" and quite another to be a rock star. Wasn't this the most coveted career a young man could have in America in the twenty-first century? Rock stars were pharaohs with an endless supply of concubines—far superior to actors or presidents or, dare he say, teachers. In the pyramid of celebrity worship, rock stars were the point at the top. Teachers weren't even at the base, but buried somewhere beneath the surface.

Saunders wondered how *he* looked to his friend. Was he revealing anything that might have clued Will in to his state of mind? To the fact that he felt suicidal? What did that face look like anyway? Had he ever seen this look on someone's face?

The early spring weather already meant continuous sunshine at least until the fall, and it was a beautiful day to be up in L.A. proper, where he hadn't been in a long time. No denying he lived in one of the most beautiful regions of the world. A place people traveled to from all over, just to bake in the sun for a week.

"So," he asked Will, "are all your teenage dreams finally realized?"

"It's hard work more than anything else, King," Will said.

The waiter came to take their drink orders, and Will ordered a mineral water.

"How about a dirty martini?" Saunders said. The waiter stood there as if waiting for him to clarify his order.

"Gin. On the rocks," he said.

"Any particular gin?"

"Well is fine."

No matter what brand he chose, all of his drinks made him "well."

"Sometimes I think, if this rock and roll stuff doesn't pan out, I might try to write a novel," Will said. "Been messing around with a few ideas. Got some connections now and I think I can get it published."

"Rock star *and* a novelist? You can't be both of those things," Saunders said.

"Why not?"

"It isn't fair."

The waiter brought the drinks. Will had never been the drinking type, but Saunders noticed he'd picked up a different type of addiction—looking at his phone.

"I mean it's not like it's the seventies or anything," Will said, still staring down at his phone. "What do you want me to say? Flying first class across the globe is great. Staying in five-star hotels is great. Talking to pretty girls is great. Getting to meet some of my idols is great. But it's not as glamorous as you might think. What about you? What have you been up to?"

What could he say? Writing suicide notes is great, getting drunk is great, teaching at two different schools is great—but not as glamorous as you might think.

"I should have learned how to play guitar," Saunders said.

They laughed and began to reminisce about the old days in community college—particularly the time Will had failed to show up to their Intro to Literature class for a presentation he was supposed to give on Emily Dickinson.

"I'd still rather stand in front of a stadium full of 30,000 people any day than give a presentation on Emily Dickinson," Will said.

He ordered a steak and Saunders said he would just drink, figuring the cost of the drinks alone would be expensive.

"Dude," Will said. "We're at Musso's. Get a steak."

And when it came, did it ever taste good. Rare and juicy, fulfilling all his primal urges. Some of them, anyway.

Saunders looked around the restaurant. Quite an extravagant crowd even at lunch. The waiters, all in their bowties and red jackets, went around presenting everyone with wine menus. He wondered how much money they took home in a year. He wondered if Musso's was hiring.

"So what happened?" Will said. The conversation had turned to the subject of Kathy.

"I've been trying to figure that out," Saunders said. "Maybe things just ran their course."

"I always thought you could do better," Will said.

But Will really wasn't that interested. He had asked out of obligation. He was distracted and kept looking down at his phone. Someone kept texting him throughout their lunch.

Saunders noticed a rather sturdily built older man with blondish white hair, a NASA cap, and wearing a ton of jewelry, alongside a petite skinny woman entering the restaurant and being taken to a booth behind them.

"Not to be random or anything," Saunders said, "but isn't that Buzz Aldrin?"

Will tried to look behind him and then shrugged. He seemed unimpressed.

"Dude," Saunders said. "That's the second motherfucker on the moon."

Maybe there was one thing you could be that really was *more* rock star than even a rock star.

Will laughed.

"Second," he said.

He had a point. What did it mean to be the second man on the moon? To live your life knowing that in the best thing you'd accomplished, you'd come in second place.

Saunders once read that Buzz was thirty-nine when he walked on the moon. That his mother had committed suicide only weeks before. That when he came back, he'd worked as a car salesman and was suicidal himself. If it wasn't enough to be the second man on the moon in America, how could it possibly be enough to be a part-time English teacher?

"I mean, you don't really believe that, do you?" Will said.

"Believe what?"

"That we landed on the moon."

Saunders was on his second martini by this time, but he wasn't drunk enough to have misheard him.

"Are you kidding?" Saunders said.

"I mean," Will said, "don't you think it's kinda funny that we never went back?"

"We did go back," Saunders said. "Like six times."

"I don't know, man," Will said. "I just don't think it really hap-pened."

It was like talking to Adam. Had everybody suddenly lost their minds?

"Maybe you should ask Buzz," Saunders said, suddenly remembering how a few years earlier Buzz Aldrin had punched somebody in the face who'd called him a liar at a press conference.

But just then they were interrupted by the busboy.

"I'm really sorry to bother you," he said to Will. "But can I get a picture?"

Will looked at Saunders and smirked.

"Sure, King," he said, standing up.

The busboy handed Saunders his phone to take the picture.

"I love the new album," he said to Will.

"Thanks," Will said.

But do you see the guy behind you? Saunders wanted to shout at the kid as he snapped the picture. You know the second man to walk on the fucking moon?

"And another thing," Will said, after he'd sat back down, continuing the conversation. "Who took the picture of Armstrong stepping onto the moon?"

"Are you out of your mind?" Saunders's voice had gotten louder. The drinks had fulfilled their role. A couple people turned to look at their table. Embarrassed, Will lowered his voice.

"Relax, dude," he said. "I'm fucking with you."

When they finished eating their steaks, the waiter came and took their plates and Will asked for the check.

"Do you mind taking me back?" Will said. "I gotta get some sleep before the gig tonight."

When the waiter brought the bill, Will put his card down.

"I know what you do for a living," he said, pushing away Saunders's hand. Though Saunders feigned wanting to pay his fair share, he was secretly relieved to let Will pay, all the while wondering if this would be the last time he'd ever see his friend.

CHAPTER 37
Support Services

Saunders walked into the mailroom to find his path blocked by Tom Corona, down on one knee, getting his face licked by some kind of three-legged terrier. The dog belonged to a colleague of theirs, Misty Peterson, who taught Reading.

He had so many questions at that moment. Not only what was a three-legged dog doing in the mailroom, but what was Tom Corona doing down on one knee letting the dog make out with him?

"He's my emotional support dog," Misty said.

"Your what?" Saunders asked.

"My emotional support dog. He helps keep me calm."

"You haven't had any emotional support pets in class yet, Berlin?" Tom said. "It's the new thing. I've had a couple. I make sure they're always welcome. Nothing looks better on a resume than some kind of honorable mention from Disabilities Services."

"No," Saunders said.

"Yes, you are a good boy," Tom said, scratching under the terrier's chin.

"Berlin, you and Misty know each other, don't you?"

"We've seen each other around, I'm sure," Saunders said. He'd bumped into her in the mailroom over the last twelve years though he couldn't remember ever really talking to her. She wasn't very memorable with thick eyebrows, blotchy red skin, brown hair tied back in a bun that looked like it hadn't been washed or combed in years.

"And this little guy is Trotsky," Tom said, squatting down once again to pet the dog.

"Trotsky, huh?" Saunders said, annoyed by the social pressure to indulge people's pets, as he attempted to squat down and touch the dog's head.

"Hi there, Trotsky."

But the pathetic little creature growled at him. Okay then. Saunders stood up.

"Maybe not," he said.

"He's still getting used to people," Misty told him.

"Maybe the emotional support dog needs an emotional support dog," Saunders joked.

All of them laughed except Trotsky who hobbled on its three little tiny legs across the floor and bit Saunders right in his shin. At first, he just felt a little pinch and wasn't even sure the dog bit him.

"Trotsky!" Misty screamed. She swept the creature up with one hand and dropped him into her purse where the dog looked at Saunders, still growling.

"I'm really sorry," she said.

"It's nothing," Saunders told her. "Just a pinch."

She left soon after and Saunders walked over to his mailbox.

"I think we have a vibe," Tom said.

"Who does?"

"Me and Misty," Tom said. "Excuse me—Misty and I."

"I thought you meant you and Trotsky," Saunders said.

"Very funny."

"You like her?" Saunders asked.

"I could," Tom said. "I mean she's not exactly my type. I've always imagined myself with someone a little, well…" Tom couldn't say it.

"Better looking?" Saunders said.

Tom looked around as if making sure they were still alone.

"Not that I'm sexist or anything," he said.

Saunders reached down and pulled up the pant leg of his jeans. There were two little dots of blood where Trotsky had attacked. *Motherfucker.* Damn crippled commie dog. Should have named him Stalin.

"Who am I kidding, anyway?" Tom said, looking once again around the room as if someone had secretly entered and he hadn't noticed. Saunders wondered where the snorer was. "It's not like I can even afford to take care of myself these days."

"Heard anything about the WAC job yet?"

"Nothing. Don't you think I should have by now?"

"No news is good news. Isn't that how the cliché goes?"

"But certainly they must be holding second interviews by now?"

"You know how it is," Saunders said. "It takes a long time for this school to do anything."

"Yeah," Tom said, wiping sweat off his forehead with a paper towel from a roll he kept in his bag. "Can't give up. I'll just have to apply again next year. Don't want to be stuck at you-know-where forever. Gotta stay positive, right?"

Saunders didn't believe Tom for a second. The disappointment had drained his face of any color and Saunders regretted bringing the position up at all. Maybe at one point it had bothered him that he wouldn't be picked for full-time work, but not in the way it bothered Tom who looked about to cry. If they were women, Saunders would have hugged him.

"Men can't hug each other?" Kathy said to him one time. The truth is he had gotten used to giving men hugs, it was just that there had been times he'd given a hug to a man who hadn't expected it and the whole thing had been awkward.

Maybe she had been right. But still, he wasn't going to give Tom a hug. For one, Tom was just too sweaty. In some ways, it was sad to think that poor Tom, having been alone ever since he'd known him, probably hadn't felt a hug in a long time, much less had sex with anyone. And he definitely wasn't fucking Tom.

"I'm sure you'll hear back," Saunders said.

"Do you really think?"

"Absolutely," Saunders said. "You're the man for the job."

"Thanks, Berlin," Tom's face perked up.

What use was it to tell him the truth? No matter how much he kissed ass, Tom was never going to be offered the WAC job. He was too awkward, not always the most personable, probably a bad lecturer, and as previously stated, sweaty. No matter how many committees he sat on, he was doomed to be an adjunct like the rest of them; he just hadn't realized it yet.

Saunders dug his hand into his mailbox and pulled out a pile of papers accrued since he'd last been there. Hidden within the junk flyers for theater productions and other campus events he'd never attend was a manila envelope with his name on it. He knew exactly what it was. He tossed the rest of the junk mail in the trash and opened the envelope.

Long Beach Community College

<u>Peer Evaluation Form</u>

<u>Evaluatee: Berlin Saunders</u>

1. **Participates in college committee work/activities**

    Needs Improvement

2. **Organizes classroom activities effectively**

    Needs Improvement

3. **Adapts appropriate methods and materials of teaching to meet the needs of students consistent with the maintenance of quality education**

    Needs Improvement

4. **Answers students' questions appropriately**

    Needs Improvement

5. **Material taught in class is appropriate to the course description**

    Needs Improvement

6. **Cultivates a courteous, respectful, and professional environment**

    Needs Improvement

Overall Rating: *Unsatisfactory*

"What the fuck?" he said.

Never before had he received such a rating. For the past twelve years, all had been *Satisfactory*. All that had "needed improvement" had been outside the realm of his job. The general consensus for evaluations had always been that as long as violence didn't occur in your class, you were guaranteed a *Satisfactory* rating.

Comments:

April 20

On Monday, March 24, I observed Mr. Saunders in his English 100 class. When I arrived, Mr. Saunders was in a discussion of Martin Luther King's "Letter from a Birmingham Jail," a text that is usually recommended to be cross-referenced with "Power Proposals" (see Chapter 10 of our department textbook Au Revoir, Strunk and White). Instead, Mr. Saunders led the students through an unenthusiastic discussion of some of the main points of King's letter without ever providing enough instruction or context as to the relevance of why they were studying it. As far as I could tell, the reading of this essay was not related to a specific assignment. Mr. Saunders's casual manner with his students, also, at times, seemed more like that of an acquaintance or friend than one of an authority figure. I would recommend that Mr. Saunders work a bit more on the control of his classroom as there was also a temporary distraction of an inappropriate student response to a question met by Mr. Saunders with no reprimanding. In conclusion, Mr. Saunders's demeanor demonstrates the need for further evaluation in the upcoming semester.

A blue sticky note on top said *Scheduled Meeting 5/5.*

Saunders stuffed the evaluation in his bag and snapped it.

"You know they eloped over spring break," Tom said.

"What?" Saunders said. "How do you know?"

Tom pointed to Kathy's box. The full-timers' boxes were separate from the adjuncts' boxes just like everything else. Then he saw it: *Kathy Crawford-Stone.*

"I saw them changing the sticker the other day," Tom said.

So she had agreed to hyphenate her name? Something she'd sworn never to do. In fact, already, she had done a lot of firsts that with him she'd always said she wouldn't. Impossible to think Kathy had taken Crawford's name even if it was hyphenated.

"It's the narrative of slavery," she'd once told Saunders. "Why should a woman lose her identity just because she gets married?" How had she changed her mind then? How had she taken on the master's name? She even let Crawford put his name before hers.

"He did it too," Tom said.

Saunders looked down at his bag for a second and then unsnapped it and pulled out the evaluation. *Harry Crawford-Stone.* How had he missed this?

"Hitler's fucking birthday," Saunders said, the date on his evaluation sinking in.

He started to shove the papers back into his bag.

"Are you quitting?" Tom said. "I guess you can give me your bag then."

Saunders thought about it and then held the bag up and started shaking everything out of it: Dry erase markers, paperclips, mechanical pencils, old check stubs, a pair of cheap sunglasses.

"I was just joking," Tom said, arms raised and palms facing out from his chest. "What are you doing?"

"What am I doing?" Saunders said. "I'm giving you my bag."

"But no, I can't—," Tom said, still looking around, keeping his hands up, and stepping back as if not wanting to be some kind of accomplice. "There's still two weeks of class left. What will you use?"

"Consider it a parting gift," Saunders said, keeping the bag upside down until twelve years' worth of paper clips that had defied gravity until now fell to the ground.

"But—," Tom said.

"I won't offer again," Saunders said, shoving the bag rather violently at Tom. "Take it."

"Well," Tom said, taken aback at first, but after turning it over in his head suddenly smiling at the gift Saunders had just shoved at him. "Okay. You know I've always loved this bag."

"I'm glad it'll be in good hands," Saunders said, picking up the mess he'd made after dumping everything out and throwing it all in the trashcan.

"How are you going to carry all your stuff?" Tom asked.

"I'll figure it out," he said, looking around the room. "There's only two weeks left."

"Here," Tom said, methodically emptying out his own bag, "at least take mine."

He handed Saunders his own empty bag and pulled out his phone. "And put my number in your contacts."

Saunders agreed.

"In case of emergency," Tom said.

CHAPTER 38

TARGET AUDIENCE

"I don't know how to shoot a gun," was all Saunders told Adam.

"I knew you'd come to your senses," Adam said.

His truck was spotless, gleaned in the streetlights, which had just come on when he'd picked Saunders up at his apartment. The paint job looked freshly waxed, the inside vacuumed, not a dust mote anywhere to be found on the dash. Compared to his own car, with half the fender falling off (after a hit and run in the neighborhood last summer), the crack across the windshield, the unwashed desert dust of Southern California caked all over the black body, the receipts from fast food restaurants on the floor, the empty cigarette boxes, Adam's car was luxurious.

"Where are we going?" Saunders said.

"Relax," Adam said. "We're going to see an old friend of mine. Just a little target practice."

How much of an old friend could one have at Adam's age? Saunders felt the twitch in his left eye return.

By the time midnight came, they were out past Edwards Air Force Base.

They ended up in Kern County, driving down a long dirt road, the headlights the only two lights in a world of darkness. The truck bounced along the road. If it broke down now, they'd be miles away from anything or anyone. Saunders checked his cell phone. No service. Even the AAA card in his wallet was useless.

He rolled his window down and lit a smoke. He stuck his head out and looked up at the night sky. With the terrain, the endless stars, the Milky Way right above his head, the criminal intent, he felt like a character in a Cormac McCarthy novel.

Soon they arrived at a house with only a single light on in the window. Adam parked his truck in the dirt on the side of the road and they stepped out. He pulled the truck's seat forward and from behind pulled out a rifle case and a smaller case that looked like it was for a handgun. He handed the smaller one to Saunders.

A tall ethnically-indeterminate looking guy named Hartley gave Adam a half hug and hard pat on the back. Then he held out his big hand to shake Saunders's hand.

"What is this?" he said to Adam, noting Saunders's blazer, "a poetry seminar?"

They had a good laugh at Saunders's expense and then Hartley said, "Professor. Welcome."

They walked into an impressive single-story house, very neat and orderly. Though Saunders couldn't identify what type of furniture was in there, he knew it wasn't from Ikea—expensive stuff imported with expensive shipping costs. A leather couch and chair and the walls were covered with paintings Saunders liked, almost abstract modernist work with some kind of Southwestern vibe. Abstract Kandinsky-like circles with bright reds, yellows, and blues. On the end tables were pictures of family members, some black-and-white oldies and some new.

Hartley brought out three cans of beer and handed one to

Saunders. They cracked them open at the same time. Saunders began to relax.

"You probably want to take a load off before we go outside. It's been a long drive," Hartley said.

"There's been longer ones," Adam said.

"Shit," Hartley said. "Guess it goes a lot faster when you don't think you might get your arms blown off every minute."

He took a sip of the beer. He was a few years older than Adam, maybe even closer to Saunders's age, but seemed far too young to have already exiled himself to the middle of nowhere.

How did Adam know Hartley? Had they been to Iraq together? Suddenly Saunders thought of how cool it was to sit there with a real Native American. All of his white liberal friends would be jealous—there was no one they fetishized more. Native Americans were their favorite indigenous group.

He assumed Hartley had been in the military with Adam. Of course, his inner white liberal couldn't resist pointing out the irony of the Native American being deployed to fight for the same government that had wiped out his people.

"You white liberals always get us Indians wrong. Most Indians are pretty conservative," Hartley said. "War is a virtue. And we love guns. Which is not to say we'll be signing any treaties anytime soon."

He laughed, then crushed his can of beer.

"But we'll save that argument for another day," said Hartley. "Ready to go out back?"

They followed Hartley out into the backyard and after walking for a while came upon a chain link fence with a gate and a sign on it: NO TRESPASSING.

"History has taught me one thing," he said, pointing to the sign.

He unlocked the gate and they stepped through. Hartley squatted down near a rigid electrical box, like the kind you might find on a construction site, and flipped on two large spotlights. About twenty feet in front of them were two paper targets, both human silhouettes.

"Illegal in civilian shooting ranges," he told them.

Beside the range stood a small shed.

They followed Hartley in. Three card tables were lined up against the wall with a stockpile of guns, all different sizes and of all different calibers. Next to the tables were belts of ammunition, and a few other more dangerous launcher-looking things that Saunders didn't even want to begin thinking about.

"The explosives you asked for are over there," Hartley said, pointing to a box on the edge of one table.

Adam walked over to the table.

"You know how to assemble them?" Hartley asked.

What did they need explosives for?

"I've done my research," Adam said.

Adam looked at Hartley, then clutched onto the rifle case he'd slung around his shoulder.

"Anything else? Ammo?" Hartley said. "A rifle for the professor?"

Adam laughed.

"I got plenty of guns. And ammo I can get cheaper at Walmart," he said, winking at Hartley.

The three men stood about twenty feet away from the human targets.

One of the first steps to getting started on a piece of writing is to identify your target audience.

"You'll need these," Hartley said, handing Saunders earplugs and glasses. "Always wear ear and eye protection regardless of whether you are shooting or not."

It made sense. There were a lot of things he didn't want to see and didn't want to hear.

Despite the earplugs, his ears burst and rang immediately at the pop from Adam's trigger. A strong smell of sulfur lodged up his nose as he saw a puff of smoke come out of Adam's gun. This was not a shooting gallery at an amusement park where your target lights up. This was no trip to Knott's Berry Farm.

"Watch the firing line," Hartley said, pulling Saunders back a bit as Adam prepared to take his next shot.

Saunders couldn't resist thinking that'd be a great title for a book on writing.

The Firing Line: How to Write a Killer Research Paper

By Berlin Saunders

Chapter 1: "Loaded" - On the overuse of loaded and pretentious terminology and phrases

Chapter 2: "Triggers" - On prewriting and finding inspiration

Chapter 3: "Misfires" - Common errors

Chapter 4: "Target Audiences" – Choosing your reader

Chapter 5: "Bullet points" – Supporting your thesis

When it was Saunders's turn, Hartley went into an extensive explanation of the right way of loading and unloading his weapon.

Think of prewriting like loading a gun.

"First, never let the muzzle cover anything you are not willing to destroy," he said. "Keep your finger off the trigger. Be sure of your target and what is beyond it first before you take your stance. Verify you have the right ammunition."

Loading the wrong ammunition in your firearm is extremely dangerous, like choosing the wrong sources for your research paper. Check both the labeling on the box (i.e. credible sources), and if you're not sure get some expert advice.

"Then, once everything is in place, shoot," Hartley said, as he stepped away.

Saunders squeezed the trigger, felt the recoil as the bullet left the chamber. He missed the target completely, but felt proud of his ability to take something he learned and apply it right away.

CHAPTER 39

Make-Up Policy

Except for his brief visit with Ray Zapata, all semester Saunders had been avoiding the fourth floor of the Humanities building where the full-time faculty offices were located. But on that day, he had important matters at hand. He felt his left eye begin to twitch. For the past week, ever since he'd dumped out his bag and shoved it at Tom Corona, his eye had twitched constantly. In class. At home. But nothing made him feel as nervous as he felt right now.

He turned down the hall and could hear the voices of different faculty members talking to students, or on the phone, or talking to each other. On the walls were pictures of famous writers who had written in English: Whitman, Melville, Dickinson, Updike, even a picture of Hemingway someone had defaced. He knew this route, as he had taken it many times before. It only surprised him why he was doing it right then.

The door was shut. A poster for the new edition of *Au Revoir* along with a picture of a smiling middle-aged Simone De Beauvoir were both tacked on the outside. Just above them, a placard that read Professor Katherine Stone.

What was he doing there? It wasn't too late. He could still turn around. He noted how the placard didn't yet reflect her hyphenated married name. Maybe everything about love was hyphenated. Neither of them had ever really given themselves over to the other.

But here he was. He had checked her office hours before

coming and his first instinct was relief at the sight of the closed door. He noted the metaphoric implications. He was a few minutes early still. He didn't believe in closure really. Was this even that? What did he hope to achieve by seeing her face again? What was he going to say to her? These would be his last words. Was he there to make peace of some sort? No. None of that really. And what if she were to open up this door to her office and profess her love to him and tell him it was all a mistake? Would he stop this madness? He laughed at the word "profess."

What did it mean to be a "professor"? All these names: professor, instructor, lecturer. A lecture was what you got when you'd been bad as a kid. And the lecturer was the authority figure who gave you that lecture. Do all your assignments, follow all the rules, and you may just get an "A." This had been his motto for twelve years. When in fact, many of these students could work their asses off, and never earn an "A." Others entered the class with an "A" because they were already good writers and left with an "A" having hardly worked at all. Well, he was tired of being a lecturer. He wanted to be the bad kid.

Saunders knocked.

Behind the door, he heard some movement, the squeak of a chair, the setting of a cup on a desk, and then the turning door handle. In front of him stood the woman he once loved, or thought he loved; he wasn't really sure at this point what love even meant anymore. He'd expected she'd look good to him now that she couldn't be his, but what he hadn't expected was that familiar citrusy scent of her perfume.

"Berlin," she said, thrown off by his knocking on her office door, no doubt expecting him to be a student or someone else she'd be more comfortable welcoming.

"You got a minute?" he said.

Kathy hesitated, skeptical of his being there. They hadn't said a word to each other in four months. The question should have been, "Have you got a minute to talk to *me*?"

She looked at him, then sort of glanced sideways down the hall as if remembering who she was and where they were.

"I have a student coming," she said. "But sure. I have a couple minutes."

She shut the door behind him. The first thing he noticed were balloons orbiting above her desk that said *Congratulations*. On top of the desk was a bouquet of flowers. From Harry, no doubt. When was the last time Saunders had given her flowers? He had tried to be romantic, hadn't he? For no occasion, sometimes, he'd shown up at home with flowers for her. She liked a kind called Stargazers that he'd bought at Trader Joe's for eight bucks when they'd first started dating. The flowers didn't last very long. Usually, by the next day, he'd wake up to a pile of petals around the bottom of the vase. But these flowers were more elaborate: Colorful, fresh, expensive. Meant to last.

Kathy sat down at her desk and Saunders in the chair next to her usually reserved for students. He'd brought a gift with him. A hardcover copy of Charlotte Perkins Gilman's autobiography he'd ordered on Amazon Prime (which he got for free with his school ID). He wanted to make her laugh and she did.

"You're ridiculous," she said, smiling. But she took it and set it on her desk next to a pile of papers.

"Thankfully, there aren't any pictures," he joked. "But you still owe me a new shirt."

She looked at him with sympathetic eyes as if he were a struggling student. Could she help him develop his thesis a bit? Maybe point him in the direction of finding good sources? Write him a letter of recommendation? He felt as nervous as he did when on occasion he'd visited one of his own professors in college. Except that four months ago, he'd heard this professor snore in bed. He'd cleaned her hair out of the shower drain. Her toothpaste off the bottom of the bathroom sink. He'd taken her temperature. Brought her water when she was throwing up. Some mornings he'd woken up with his chest against her back. She'd called him embarrassing pet names like "bunny" and they'd watched porn together. And still, somehow, they were two strangers sitting there. That had been expected, but he hadn't expected one of them to still be clinging to something. In a way, for the first time, he realized it wasn't him. It was her. The way she said, "You're ridiculous." The look she'd given that seemed to say, *Why didn't you fight for me?*

It's true he hadn't fought for her. His pride wouldn't let him. She betrayed their relationship and he saw no point in trying to save it. A different man might have felt less hopeless about it. He had friends who'd suffered similar fates and considered themselves victorious for salvaging the hearts of their cheating mates. His unwillingness to fight for her was something even he wondered about. But it was all too late to ponder anything now. He'd shown up at her office hours for something else entirely. He had come to say goodbye.

"Things ended so abruptly," he said. "I just wanted to..."

"It's okay," Kathy said. "I don't think either one of us can find the right words to explain what happened. But I appreciate your coming here. It means a lot to me."

"For what it's worth," Saunders said, "it was a good five years."

"Yes, it was," Kathy said.

"I guess I should also tell you congratulations," Saunders said.

"How did you know?" Kathy said.

"Tom."

"Of course," she said. "I hope he's not gonna be too upset."

"Upset?" Saunders said. "Why would Tom be upset about you eloping?"

Kathy looked at him.

"Oh that," she said, putting her hands on her lap and smoothing out her dress. "I'm sorry. I should have told you myself."

"It's not necessary," Saunders said.

"You know how bendy love is," she said.

Bendy? She would have never used such a fatuous word before. It sounded like something straight out of Crawford's book. Chapter 20 in *Au Revoir*: Bendy verbs. It made him sick.

"What were *you* talking about?" Saunders asked, curious now as to why all the confusion.

Kathy leaned back in her chair and glanced at her computer monitor, then back at him with a smile.

"I'm the new WAC coordinator," she said.

CHAPTER 40
Signal Phrases

"You never check your email, do you?" Tom Corona said when he called Saunders at seven the next morning.

"Sorry," Saunders said, still trying to wake up. What could possibly be so urgent that Tom would be calling this early on a Saturday? Then he remembered what Kathy told him. Maybe he had heard. News or not, nothing justified waking him up this early on a Saturday.

"What is it?" Saunders said.

"I need to talk to you about something," Tom said.

"We are talking," Saunders said. He yawned and walked into his kitchen to make coffee. He wouldn't go back to sleep now.

"I mean in person," he said.

"Can't it wait?" Saunders asked.

"Better you hear it from me first," he said.

What was he talking about? If he did find out, wasn't *he* the one who needed to talk? Saunders worried about Tom. Though Tom had been the one to insist they exchange numbers, Saunders had never intended to use his.

"I'll meet you at the coffee shop in twenty minutes," Tom said.

"Which coffee shop?" Saunders asked.

"The one beneath your apartment," Tom said, then swiftly hung up, not giving Saunders a chance to deny or confirm. How did Tom know where he lived? Sure, they occupied the same neighborhood, but he'd never told him exactly where before. Somehow, it didn't surprise him either. Might as well forgo the coffee. He'd get some downstairs.

By the time he got there, Tom was sitting inside waiting for him. Saunders bought some coffee from the skinny Asian owner, then asked Tom if he minded moving to a table in front where he could smoke.

"Do you feel like you're cheating on your other job?" he joked, coming awake finally.

"Very funny," Tom said.

An insensitive comment given the likelihood Tom would have to keep working at that other job.

The sun had already burned away the marine layer and though it was only a couple days into May, it felt like summer already—a summer he was never going to see.

Saunders yawned and lit a smoke, certain whatever Tom had to tell him could have waited.

"He lied," Tom said, reaching into Saunders's old bag and pulling out a manila folder.

What had he expected? Tom needed the kick-in-the-ass. For too long he had been worshipping at the altar of King Crawford and it was time to revolt. Maybe Tom could really be an ally now. If it wasn't already too late.

"Don't have to convince me," Saunders said. "I've been trying to warn you about Crawford for a long—."

"Not Crawford," Tom said. "Adam Rowan."

"Adam?" said Saunders. "What do you mean?"

"I couldn't resist," Tom said, placing the manila folder on the table. "I was about to give him the scholarship, but then I put it through Copycat."

"What's this?" Saunders asked, opening the manila folder handed to him.

"It's an originality report," Tom said. "According to the similarity index, Adam's paper is in the 80th percentile. I sent you a PDF, but you don't check your emails, apparently."

"What does that mean? The 80th percentile?" Saunders asked.

"It means you have a plagiarizer on your hands," Tom said. "Plain and simple."

"An 80% plagiarizer," Saunders said, still courting his denial, "which means 20% is his own."

Tom looked at him.

"I guess," he said. "If you want to see the cup 20% full."

Was Adam capable of this? And what did it mean if Adam had lied 80% of the time in his paper? Did it mean his war experience had been 80% fraudulent and only 20% true? And which 20%? Had he made the whole thing up? And if he could lie to him about this, what else was he lying about?

"Be proud," Tom said, putting his hand on Saunders's shoulder. "We caught a bad guy."

"Let me read this," Saunders said.

The usual slew of dog walkers passed them, as did the weekend joggers. Morning traffic was building on the street. Where was everybody going? Saunders grabbed his pack off the table for another cigarette. It probably wasn't even 8 o'clock yet, but he already knew he'd smoke a lot that day.

He looked down at the papers in the folder. There was some of Adam's text, highlighted with various percentages off to the side.

"Originality report," Saunders said. "If we're rating papers by originality then all my students would fail."

In truth, he felt nervous. How had Adam duped him like this? Or was foolishness just a basic character trait he had inherited from his unknown dad? Obviously, his father had been foolish enough to knock his mother up.

The originality report Tom had given him included highlighted parts from the text that matched a source on the Internet.

"But just to be sure the computer was correct, I did my own search and it brought me to this."

He reached over and grabbed the folder back, then flipped through a couple pages, took the paper clip off one of his printouts, and handed it to Saunders. It was text from some vet's anti-war blog called *Lying Bastard*:

I'm only twenty, I said to God, Don't let me fucking die before I can legally drink! Not in Iraq. Not even in Paris. I wondered if God heard my plea, and then decided that He probably fucking didn't with all the gunfire and explosions all around. I wasn't too sure if He existed in the first place, but figured it probably wasn't the best time to be questioning it.

"And just in case you haven't read it lately," detective Tom said, pulling out another sheet and handing it to him, "here's Adam's version."

Verbatim. But did this mean Adam hadn't been to Iraq? That

his friend hadn't died? That he hadn't been injured? Or just that he'd cheated?

"What about his other essays?" Tom asked. "You might want to run them through."

But there weren't any other essays. Tired of grading hundreds of papers, he had scaled down his assignments to only two out-of-class essays and one final written exam each semester. Their second paper, a research essay, wasn't due until the end of the semester next week.

The denouncing highlights continued throughout Adam's paper, but Saunders stopped halfway. What did it matter now? Sure, Adam wouldn't win the scholarship, but he never knew it had been submitted in the first place. Saunders knew one thing though: he was done with this craziness. He needed to talk to Adam. And he needed to keep Tom Corona quiet about this.

"I'll talk to him," Saunders said. "How about we forget we ever had this conversation?"

Tom pulled the paper towel roll out of his bag and ripped a piece off, then wiped some sweat from his forehead.

"And you really ought to see a doctor about that," Saunders said.

"I'm just overheated," Tom said, avoiding eye contact with him. He was clearly agitated. More nervous than Saunders thought he should have been at that moment. And then Saunders realized why.

"You told Crawford, didn't you?" Saunders said.

Tom pulled another sheet off and patted the sides of his face.

"Well, Berlin, you know, I had to think about the WAC job," Tom said.

"Damn it, Tom," Saunders said, pounding the table.

"The school pays a lot of money to have Copycat," Tom said. He attempted to retrieve the manila folder from Saunders by sliding it back across the table towards him. "And I don't want to work at Starbucks forever."

"There is no job, Tom," Saunders said, slamming his fist down on the folder. "You hear me? There's no fucking job."

Tom lifted his hand away from the folder and unexpectedly reached for one of Saunders's cigarettes.

"What do you mean?" he asked, grabbing the lighter off the table.

"Kathy's the new WAC coordinator," Saunders said. "I just saw her yesterday."

Tom didn't say anything. He snubbed out the cigarette after one puff, lifted his bag up onto his lap, and snapped the buckles.

"They're planning to take disciplinary action," he told Saunders, before standing up and walking away.

CHAPTER 41
Pier Review

Saunders's cigarette smoke rose up into the ocean air where it orbited above Adam's head like that *Congratulations* balloon above Kathy's desk.

"Count me out," he said.

They met at the end of the Belmont pier, which projected out from a dead shore, waves looted years ago by oil companies who'd built a breakwater in order to drill. Nobody swam in the Long Beach ocean. Its calm coast consisted of nothing but trash and sewage that drifted in and never drifted back out. But crowds of poor Mexican and Filipino men and their families still fished off the pier, some for sport, some for dinner. The wooden planks were covered with the blood and guts of tiny fish tossed in white buckets and it smelled. Some of the men brought old radios with large antennas, some came on bikes, some drove in old trucks. He had once heard about a man who had fallen off the edge of the pier into the water and lived while the hero who jumped in to save him drowned. That's kind of how he felt right now. Hadn't he submitted Adam's paper with the best intentions? Had he not been trying to be some kind of a hero? Hadn't he also fallen off the edge? He didn't care much for drowning either. All that suffocation. People claimed it was a peaceful way to go, but no one who drowned had ever been able to verify that.

"I was never really convinced you were in," Adam said.

"Why's that?" Saunders asked.

"Because the difference between me and you, Professor Saunders, is that maybe I can't always find the words, but that's all people like you seem to have."

"You had enough words to lie to me, Adam," Saunders said.

"You said it didn't matter if we told the 100% truth about our experience," he said. "You told us we could make stuff up."

"I said you could lie, not steal," Saunders said. The words fell like dust out of his mouth. He hated the sound of his own voice.

And yet, hadn't stealing been the plan? Was he really surprised? Was it the intentions behind stealing that mattered or the stealing itself?

"You said 'reality isn't always as interesting as what we make up,'" Adam told him. "I wrote it in my notes."

It was true he did tell this to the class. And in the past, he'd even told them to steal, quoting T.S. Eliot's famous dictum, "good writers, borrow; great writers steal." He wondered what ultimately disappointed him more—that Adam lied or that he wasn't the writer Saunders wanted him to be.

"You betrayed my trust," Saunders said.

"Funny coming from someone who submitted my paper behind my back," Adam said.

"Somebody's paper, anyway," Saunders said. "My intentions were good."

"So were mine," Adam said.

"I don't see it," Saunders said.

"I was ashamed," Adam said. "Thought you'd look down on

me if I didn't write something good. I wanted you to think I was a great writer."

"Bullshit. I thought you didn't care about that," Saunders said.

"I wanted to be your friend," Adam said.

Out in the ocean were fake islands with palm trees the oil companies had built to disguise the ugliness of the wells. To their right, some distance away, the Queen Mary where Kathy had thrown Saunders a birthday party the first year they were together. Beyond that, the Los Angeles port and the large cranes like robotic dinosaurs sticking out everywhere. From where he stood, he couldn't see the Vincent Thomas Bridge, but he knew it was there. Maybe he wasn't so afraid of heights.

"Have you ever wished you were someone else?" Adam said, putting his hands on the wooden rail and staring out at one of the fake islands.

In the haze off in the distance, a line of ships waited to enter the port. On a clear day, you could see as far as Catalina. Though he'd lived in Southern California all his life, he'd never been there, much less desired to go.

"It's not good to be envious, Adam," Saunders said. "Remember your Emerson: 'Envy is suicide'?"

Of course, he was lying. He'd been envious of others most of his life. He'd even been envious of Adam. But he was also suicidal.

"Maybe it was easier for Emerson not to be envious," Adam said. "He was a genius who had a purpose in life. What do you do when you're not a genius and you've got no purpose? You're not anything. What do you do when the most you can expect is mediocrity until you die?"

A good question that had gotten him into all this mess in the first place. It wasn't enough anymore to be just a person. To be mediocre. To die without accomplishing greatness. You had to be distinguished. You had to win awards and get promotions. It wasn't enough to hold down a job anymore—you had to prosper. This is why none of his students was satisfied with a "C" anymore. Nobody wanted to be average. Nobody wanted an average grade much less an average life. Love is "bendy," after all. Isn't that what Kathy had told him? Nobody wanted a love that was a straight line. Nobody wanted an average love.

"What else have you been lying about?" Saunders asked.

"I've always been honest with you," Adam said.

"Did you even go to Iraq?" he asked.

Adam looked hurt by this question. But he had to ask, didn't he? It was on his mind and there was nothing now he could trust about Adam. What if he had lied about the whole thing? Even about going to war? He was still pretty young after all. Had any other student been caught like this? What would it have mattered? What about Hakim? What about the broken bones and the six months rehabilitation consuming all the books that he'd clearly read? What about Hartley? Was it possible to have made this all up? It was one thing to plagiarize a paper, but a whole life? And yet, hadn't Saunders also been doing this all along? It was hard to say who the bigger liar was at this point.

"Would it matter either way?" Adam asked. "Would it make

me less authentic?"

"It would make you a liar," Saunders said.

"According to you, I already am that," Adam said. "What would change? And what do you care?"

In some ways, Adam was right. What would change? Maybe his anxiety. Maybe his hurt ego. But did it matter? The paper was plagiarized, but the story was real. The war was real.

"This is grounds for dismissal from the college you know," Saunders said. "The chair of the English Department has been notified already."

Why the harsh treatment? In the past, he'd simply made his students rewrite their papers in their own words. But Tom Corona had sold him out already. Still, the decision was ultimately up to Saunders. On Monday, when he met with Crawford for his evaluation meeting, he could simply smooth it all out. But this wasn't about Crawford or getting in trouble. He had been duped by this kid and he wasn't going to stand for it. This was about his ego.

"The chair?" Adam said. "You mean the guy who stole your girlfriend? I got bigger plans anyway."

"You're still going through with it?" Saunders said.

"You bet I am," Adam said.

"I could report you to the authorities."

"But you won't."

"How do you know?"

"Because you don't really believe me."

It was true. He never really had. The whole thing had seemed entirely unreal to him. Even more so now.

"Listen," Saunders said, "there are only two days left of class. Rewrite the paper in your own words and bring it to me Monday. I will take care of Crawford. Don't give up on yourself, Adam. There's a better future out there."

Adam laughed.

"Why should I believe you?" he asked Saunders.

"Because what do I have to lie about?" he said.

"You lied to me about the scholarship," Adam said.

"Well, technically— "

"And you lied to me about your father," Adam added.

This caught Saunders off guard. His natural instinct was to deny it, of course. But that was just perpetuating the lies he'd spent his whole life concocting. If he expected honesty from Adam, wasn't it time he started being honest too?

"How did you know?" he asked.

"You didn't use the first person," Adam said.

Saunders stubbed out a cigarette on the railing of the pier. On instinct, he wanted to toss it in the ocean, but the conscientious liberal in him wouldn't let him and he stuck the ashy butt in his blazer pocket.

"Sticks and stones," he said to Adam. "Monday. Think about it."

CHAPTER 42
In Conclusion

Forgive me, my friend, for the opportunity I gave you to seem as mad as I, making you fall into the error into which I fell, thinking that there were and are knights errant in the world.

Phil was right. The end of the novel depressed Saunders. And what timing to have finished it. After all, by the end, Quixote renounces everything.

"Professor," Phil said, when he walked into the bar, "long time no see."

It was true. Saunders had been avoiding the bar ever since spring break because he didn't want to run into Liz. Why was that? He'd come to like her a lot. But she threatened the clumsy foundation he'd built his life (and death) on these last few weeks.

"I finished it," he said to Phil, who bit his lip and tilted his head, then reached beneath the bar and pulled out two shot glasses.

"I told you the end was fucked up," he said, shaking his head. After pouring the ice cold Jäger into the shot glasses, he handed one to Saunders.

"Aren't they all," Saunders said. He had reached his end, hadn't he? The trigger had been pulled. Time was running out with the semester ending that week. It was Sunday night and he didn't want to face what was in front of him, starting with tomorrow's evaluation meeting with Crawford. He, too, was ready to renounce everything.

"Salud," Phil said, clicking his shot glass. "To that renouncing bastard, Don Quixote. And to your mother's children. How is your mother by the way?"

Saunders felt the cool liquid go straight back and down his throat. His mother wasn't very well. Had he simply ignored this fact when he saw her at Easter? Her memory was slipping. It wasn't just old age, it was something else. Dementia, Alzheimer's? He had formed some kind of denial around it. She needed him to acknowledge what she couldn't acknowledge herself. She needed his help. And yet, he hadn't spoken to her since.

Still early enough for the bar to be empty, Phil had the Sunday crossword puzzle out and Saunders asked if he could look at the front page of the paper.

"Such a professor," he said. "Staying informed about the world."

Not really. Just a tick he had. Empty bar or not, the big fat book he'd been carrying around for months had been his shield and he felt awkward without it.

Phil reached below the bar and pulled up the rest of the paper, the front buried in a stack of coupons. And there it was, one of the headlines:

Liberty Bell Tour Fails to Ring in a Crowd
Los Angeles Times

Though it is only a week away from completing its last stop here in Los Angeles, government officials are declaring the Liberty Bell's romp through the nation a financial disaster. With low turnout and high costs, the tour is turning out to be yet another ping in the president's armor and someone is bound to pay. Mudslinging in Washington is already taking place between the Executive and Legislative branches. Members of Congress are screaming on the gallery floors that in a year in which the government is supposed to be tightening its belt, the president's plan to reconnect Americans with their own historical legacy has been a futile endeavor.

The main issue at hand is that Americans just are not coming out in droves as the administration and the Pennsylvania governor projected.

"Maybe," suggested one senator, "after years of sinking the economy into endless war and tax breaks for the wealthy instead of job growth, they can't afford the trip."

Further evidence of the futility and stupidity of Adam's efforts. Just then, he felt a little nudge on his shoulder to the left of him, looked up, and saw Liz.

"Teacher," she said.

She had her hands on her hips in a cute, playful way.

"You said you would call."

It was true he had said that and it was just another lie in a stream of them.

"I'm sorry," Saunders said. His first instinct was to make up some reason, some lie. But he had grown sick of lying. He had been lying to himself and to everyone else for too long. What would he tell her? He had used her, and not for sex (though maybe that too), but to bring as a date to a book club? To parade in front of his colleagues as a way of telling them he'd moved on? But then something scary had happened. Sure, he'd vaguely decided to conspire to steal a national icon, but that wasn't it. The scary part was that he'd felt something for Liz.

"I forgive you, Teacher," she said, plopping down on the stool next to him. In the meantime, Phil brought her a drink and she leaned over the bar to sip her cocktail with the straw. It looked like some kind of cranberry drink. Maybe a Cape Cod or something. When he finally made eye contact, her own face was somber, sober, and caring. She picked up her drink, then clicked it against the edge of his bottle.

"We're here now."

Liz was right. She didn't mean to be, but her words were prophetic. He was still there. And for a moment, he kinda liked it.

He looked outside. He loved daylight saving time. The bar clock said it was eight which meant 7:45. The pink haze of the setting sun filtered through the tinted windows unable to keep it as dark in there as at one time he might have wanted it to be. There was a warmth in the bar that hinted of the coming summer. Maybe this was nature's trick on him? Trying to tempt him into staying in this world. The instinct to survive. The selfish gene.

"What are you thinking about, Teacher?" Liz asked.

Her big brown eyes looked up at him. The stools at 3636 were two different sizes and one had shorter legs than the other. Liz got the shorter one and it made her look much smaller than she already was.

"I'm thinking about that book I read," Saunders told her, though that wasn't exactly what he was thinking about.

"The one from the club?" Liz asked. "You finished?"

"Yes, finally," Saunders said.

"Tell the truth," Liz said, nudging him. "That's why you haven't called me, isn't it, Teacher?"

Her joke wasn't entirely off. The only difference was instead of being consumed with reading the book, he'd been consumed with living it.

"It's a sad ending," Saunders said. "The main character loses everything."

"Spoiler alert, Teacher," Liz said, nudging him once again. "Jeez."

Every time she touched him—even if it were just with her elbow—it felt good.

"Sorry," Saunders said.

"What does he lose?" Liz said.

"I thought you didn't want to know?"

"Well, too late now, Teacher."

"Everything that matters to him," Saunders said.

"Like what? His wife? His house? His children? His career? Be more specific, Teacher."

"No," Saunders said. "Worse. His idealism."

"Ah," Liz said, laughing. "I thought you were going to say something more serious. Not so sad, Teacher."

"What do you mean?" Saunders said, folding up the paper that was still in front of him. "He renounces everything. What are you without your ideals?"

Liz scratched her fingers beneath his chin.

"A human being, Teacher," she said. "You're a human being."

CHAPTER 43

Coarse Conduct

Joanne was on the phone when Saunders showed up to the English Department office Monday morning for his scheduled performance evaluation meeting. She forced a smile, held her hand over the receiver, and said, "Go on in."

Without hesitation, he walked back to Crawford's office and tapped on the open door. Crawford stood up from behind his desk and came around to shake Saunders's hand. Though he wasn't wearing the brooch this time, he wore a baseball cap and jeans with a blazer. He looked skinnier than the last time Saunders had seen him, almost gaunt, jaundiced. Maybe the cancer was somewhere in there eating away at him. On his desk sat a wedding picture of him and Kathy. On the wall, a clichéd print of Van Gogh's *Sunflowers*. The only books on the shelves were copies of the new edition of *Au Revoir*.

"Please," Crawford said, "sit."

Saunders took a seat in one of two iron chairs with torn cushions as Crawford made his way around his desk.

"I figured it'd be better to meet in person to discuss everything," Crawford said, straightening some papers on his desk. "I didn't want to just call you on the phone. It's so impersonal." After fidgeting for a bit, Crawford stopped and looked up at him.

"How's your semester going anyway?" he said.

"Almost done," Saunders said.

"Well," Crawford said, "it's a lovely time, isn't it? Any big plans for the summer?"

"Yes," Saunders said. There had been big plans all right, but none of which he could reveal to Crawford.

"I mean, sometimes, I look around this office, and I'm just amazed that this is my job," Crawford said.

The sun came in through the window as if rising behind Crawford's baseball hat and sprayed light into Saunders's eyes. He thought of Camus's *The Stranger*. *The sun was in my eyes.* Meursault's only alibi. *Meur* and *sault* together meant *to die alone.* He remembered that from a college French literature class he'd taken.

Crawford got up and closed the blinds so that Saunders could once again look him in the eye.

Just get it over with already. After all, he'd read the report. What more was there to say?

"So, like I mentioned, I figured it'd be better if we talked person to person," Crawford said. Man to man. Mano a mano. Or was it mano y mano? "It seems more and more a rare thing these days, doesn't it? People talking."

Crawford seemed to be enjoying himself too much to rush through this moment. No doubt, the highlight of his day.

"With text messaging, phones, all this online stuff for god's sake," he said. "We just seem to have lost the art of face-to face-conversation."

This was going to take longer than he wanted. There wasn't a clock in Crawford's office and Saunders's phone was in his pocket.

"And then when you think about the names of all these things," Crawford said, "i-this, i-that, my-this, my-that, Facebook. What kind of world are we, well, facing?"

Saunders thought about Adam's comment. "You didn't use the first person." A sure shot way, he claimed, to know when someone is lying. Junk science that had somehow worked with Saunders. But hadn't Adam also used "I" in his paper? And yet, he had lied.

"Do you know what I'm saying?" Crawford said.

"Sure, Harry."

"And then there's all this madness in the world, killing terrorists, warmongering, global warming. It's quite a time to be alive. But you know, all this information and… how are we supposed to digest it? You can Google anything at the touch of your hand, and yet, nobody knows anything about being wise. But you do, don't you, Berlin? You know about wisdom. You're a wise man. I've always thought that. Always thought you were one of the wise ones. Maybe it's something about your face. You know, you have one of those honest faces. Did anybody ever tell you that? One of those faces that just refuses to lie. Sometimes, I imagine, even despite your best interests. Well…," Crawford said, picking up a white mug on his desk with a picture of Yeats on it and slurping up some coffee.

"I'm sorry, how rude of me," Crawford said. "Would you like a cup?"

"No thanks," Saunders said, pulling out his phone to look at the time. "I have class in a little bit."

"There he goes again," Crawford said, as if there were a third person sitting in the empty chair next to Saunders. "The face that doesn't lie. I know this must be uncomfortable. But I admire that a lot, you know. I admire a man who can't resist speaking his mind despite his best interests. But, of course, it can get you into trouble sometimes, as I'm sure you know. The inability to resist saying what you think—I mean, imagine, if I went around saying what I think all the time. I'd be unemployed, wouldn't I? I'd be alone, wouldn't I? All this honesty in the world. It's not always the best policy. It hurts people. Don't you agree?"

Saunders nodded though his nod was a lie in itself, an almost instinctual reaction to avoid more discomfort in an already awkwardly tense situation.

"Kat mentioned you dropped by to see her Friday," Crawford said. *Kat?* "I'm really so glad you two could talk now and we can all be friends. She's an amazing woman and we've just hired her to be the new WAC coordinator, which I'm really happy about. You know it's been a knife through my heart to think of all the tension between the three of us. Who can deny it's been a wee bit uncomfortable this semester? So I'm glad to know that you've patched it all up."

The sun was in my eyes.

"Anyway," he said, smiling at Saunders, in that same smug way the president liked to smile. "Not to take up too much of your time. After all, who's got time anymore? We're always running late. Trying to fight for our time. Rushing around like little insects. Of course, Kafka wrote about this seventy years ago, didn't he? Poor Gregor Samsa. A man who had denied himself for so long, it'd take a vile metamorphosis for him to finally say no. My students always love that story. You know, I read an article by a medical doctor who wrote about Samsa like someone with a terminal disease and the burden and strain it might put on family members. I do feel sorry for old Gregor, of course. But I can't say I blame his family. After all, sometimes, if we're honest about things, some people can be a nuisance. Some people can be so vile that they put a strain on everybody else. Nonetheless, poor Gregor Samsa. It's not his fault, of course. He was just taking care of everyone. A martyr, wasn't he? We love a martyr, sometimes. Some people see themselves this way, take on this role. A way, perhaps, of convincing themselves that they're doing it for someone else. You've never done anything like that have you, Saunders?"

Saunders checked the time on his phone again.

"But anyway," Crawford said. "I digress. There I go pontificating again. So, what's going on? Everything all right in all your classes? No students giving you grief? No *martyrs*? The paper-grading level is okay?"

"Everything's fine," Saunders said.

"How's the job front?" Crawford said. "Any openings around town for full-time tenure track jobs? I'd heard of a few places hiring. You going out for any of those? I really wish we could find a way to hire everybody full time. It's really a sad state of things, don't you think? I know poor Tom Corona…well, I wish I could find something for him. But the budgets, yadda yadda yadda. I tell ya, when my reign of the English Department is over, I won't mind it at all. A couple more years and maybe it'll be time to let someone else take over. I'm ten or so years older than you, and before I retire, I think I'd like to get back full time in the classroom. Like I always say, I'm a teacher before anything else. But one thing I do want to make sure of, Saunders, is that I leave the department in good standing. That it's a better place to work than it was when I came in. That I leave a lasting legacy. It's important to make sure we're providing the best possible education to our students, wouldn't you agree?"

Saunders nodded again.

"I mean, in all these years, I've never—" Crawford said. "Well, never mind. But I must admit to being a bit shocked about a few things. But you know, some semesters go well, some go poorly. Everybody knows that. And yet, what would you do if you were in my shoes? After all, students have all the power these days. Something goes wrong in a classroom and the dean starts asking me why that is? How can I take such a risk with my job? It's not easy, Saunders, as I'm sure you can imagine. I mean, the demands of this job...trust me, you wouldn't want to be chair of the department. It's like being the president of the United States— Congress acts up, refuses to pass a bill, and who gets the blame? The economy slumps, people can't find jobs, violence breaks out in the Middle East, whose job is it to figure out what the hell to do about it? Students sign up for a course with certain expectations and we have an obligation to meet those expectations. They buy the book. And then a teacher comes along and decides he's going to break all the rules, going to teach what he wants to teach instead of what's in their textbook, comes to class disheveled and unorganized and suddenly I have the dean down my neck wondering why that is? And then, on top of it all, there's this…"

He slid a copy of Tom Corona's originality report from Adam's paper over to Saunders.

He didn't bother to take it.

"I've seen it already," he told Crawford.

"You've seen it already?" he said. "Well, then you know why I might be a little disconcerted right now."

"Listen, Harry," Saunders said. "He's a good kid. He messed up. I'll fix things."

Crawford leaned back in his chair and lifted his baseball cap to wipe off some sweat on his forehead before placing it back on.

"You know, if it were just this one thing," Crawford said, "it might not be that big of a deal. An oversight, perhaps. Hey, we're all human, aren't we? We make mistakes, don't we? I mean, I can easily see how one might fail to look into whether or not a student has plagiarized. And you might be right. Maybe Adam Rowan is a good kid. Maybe he deserves a second chance. But I'm not so sure the same rings true for his teacher."

"Are you firing me, Harry?" he said. "You can't do this."

"Well," Crawford said, "technically I can. The evaluation… adjunct…"

"I'll go to the union," Saunders said.

Crawford smiled and leaned back in his chair.

"The union," he said. "God, I love the union. Aren't they just a great organization? You know what's tragic in this country?

Unions get so little respect these days. They have such little power. I say this as a union member myself. It's really a shame how we've disarmed unions in the United States. I wholeheartedly believe in the strength of a good solid union and I hate to see it so handicapped these days. That's something we really ought to look into as faculty. What can we do to strengthen the union? Then again, you can't really blame it on the union. I mean, when's the last time you or I went to a meeting? I'm guilty as charged when it comes to the union. It's a real shame."

Saunders didn't respond to this. What about Adam? He needed to get downstairs and talk to him before it was too late.

"Anyway," Crawford said, reconsidering, perhaps even fearing the repercussions of Saunders's threat. "Here's what I'm going to do for you, Berlin. Now listen carefully: I'm going to give you a second chance next semester. I'll come in and evaluate you. We'll do this all over again. Maybe you're just going through a tough time right now. Understandably, things must be emotional for you. I know we have reason not to see eye to eye. I know you have reason to hate me, Saunders. I know you feel that I've betrayed you somehow. Both Kat and I. But let's just put the past behind us now. If things go all right next semester, I'll consider renewing your contract, but if not, I'm going to have to let you go."

Crawford held out his hand.

With that, Saunders picked up his bag and headed downstairs to the classroom, one final time.

FINAL EXAM

CHAPTER 44
Classroom Etiquette

If you are planning for a year, sow rice.
If you are planning for a decade, plant trees.
If you are planning for a lifetime, get an education.

— *Chinese Proverb*

All semester long Saunders had seen this proverb posted on the gray wall of the classroom, but it was only while lying here now, with his eyes closed, that he gave it any thought. A lifetime was much different from a life. And no amount of education had ever been able to teach him how to have one. If he were to be extinguished on this classroom floor, did it really make a difference what he had or hadn't known? Funny how similar the words "extinguished" and "distinguished" sounded. The "distinguished faculty" award was one he'd never earn. What might be the stipend for an "extinguished faculty" award?

His tongue felt lumpy and dry inside his mouth. He needed water. He'd never been so thirsty in his life. Where was the gunman now? There had to be an end to this. But whose end? His end? An end at the hands of someone else?

You tried to do it for me, Adam. But I'm still here. What did that even mean at this point? To still be here? Still in the classroom, playing dead? How long had it been? Six, eight, twelve years? Or just a few hours? Saunders had failed to convince Adam. He'd failed to be a hero. He'd even failed to kill himself.

Something moved inside the classroom.

Afraid to see what it was, he kept still. But when he felt something brush against his leg, his eyes popped open. A white fluffy rabbit stuck its twitching pink nose into his face and then sat there staring at him. Goddam rabbits. To think they shared DNA. How did it get in here? Was the classroom door still open? Could he make a run for it? Saunders tried to blow air at the creature to make it leave, but his lungs felt heavy and weak like a night of smoking too many cigarettes. Finally, it hopped away, dropping a single shit pellet on the carpet. Maybe rabbits would be the only survivors on campus. Maybe one day they'd inherit the earth after we'd made ourselves extinct. As the creature hopped away, he caught a glimpse of a desk tipped over. Then he heard footsteps and quickly shut his eyes again.

Somebody had entered. He could hear the click of the door being shut behind them. Was it Adam? He thought of his mother. Who would take care of her? Had he failed her, too? He remembered a story Adam once told him about how he'd seen grown men dying on the battlefield cry out for their mothers. You couldn't plagiarize that, could you?

A few more footsteps. Then nothing. Not a creature stirred, not even a rabbit. *Teacher, what did a rabbit ever do to you anyway?* Whoever had entered the classroom struck a match. Saunders could smell a tiny tinge of sulfur in the air, followed by cigarette smoke.

"Hi there, silly rabbit," a man's voice said.

A hand gripped Saunders's shoulder. He held his breath, but when the hand moved away, he slowly relaxed.

"I can see you breathing," the man said. He recognized the

voice. But it certainly didn't belong to Adam.

"Berlin," he said. "Berlin, for god's sake, open your eyes. I can see you breathing. Talk to me, man."

Saunders opened his eyes.

The gunman still wore the mask he'd had on earlier when he stormed into the classroom. He was down on one knee, staring at him. Through the mask, Saunders could see those familiar black pupils that always reminded him of an autistic student he once had who spent the class on his laptop making rap battles between Stewie from *Family Guy* and Bart Simpson.

"There you are," Tom Corona said, as he lifted the mask off his head. He brushed his hand back through his sweaty, thinning hair. "I can see you now." He had set two guns down on the floor next to him. Saunders didn't know what kind they were, but they looked smaller, more of the handheld type, than what he'd shot that time with Adam. Still, he couldn't move. He knew that. He couldn't grab a gun. He couldn't be a hero.

Tom's cigarette had gone out and he struck another match and then another and another.

"Fuck," he said. Tom Corona didn't smoke. He'd never seen Tom smoke until the other day. But the Tom he knew didn't murder people either. Everything was so quiet, Saunders could hear the crackling paper as Tom relit his cigarette, exhaled, then coughed. What he wouldn't give for a drag of that? It was worth the risk. Something's gotta kill you one way or another.

He realized he would probably die at the hands of the ultimate kiss-ass. Could he reason with Tom? Was there a chance he'd be spared and given back the dignity of killing himself?

"You know what the worst part is," Tom said. "I would have given my life for this shithole."

The irony is that he would. An old American tradition. When something doesn't go your way, you blow it to bits. Somehow, he wasn't surprised it was Tom. He thought of a plaque at a bar he used to go to in his twenties: Never trust a man who doesn't drink. *Never trust a man who wants tenure.* Even Tom Corona knew how to shoot a gun. Where had he learned? Maybe he'd grown up with them. Maybe he had a father who took him hunting. *Never trust a man who has a father.* In all truth, Saunders had never thought of Tom as growing up, as even being a child or having parents.

Maybe he could still do something. How many people had Tom shot? Maybe he could stop the possibility of more bloodshed. Get Tom away from his guns. Of course, none of it would bring his students back. His mouth was too dry and he wasn't even sure he could talk. His tongue had swelled to the size of an apple inside his mouth. An apple covered in dust.

"You want some of this," Tom said, holding out the cigarette. Saunders felt pins in his arm as he tried to move his hand. Tom leaned in and held the cigarette to his lips. Saunders tried to inhale, but the dryness in his mouth just made him gag.

"Look at us," Tom said, waving the smoke away from Saunders's face. "Who'd have thought things would turn out like this? Isn't life unpredictable? Here I thought I'd have my own office by now. And health benefits. And retirement. Instead, I started smoking again for Christ's sake. Another thing I can't afford. I bet you didn't know I smoked before, did you, Berlin? You probably don't care. You don't really know that much about me. Not as much as I know about you. Yeah, started in college. I had friends back then. Girls wanted to fuck me. Now I have a Ph.D. and can't even pay my rent. Pathetic. We work our asses off, only to be ignored, thrown away, exploited. Finally, we get fed up. And then we die. Let's face it, Berlin: we ain't getting out of here alive."

If Tom had been one of his students, he would have reprimanded him for his use of the first-person plural pronoun, "we," which sought to include him in this mayhem. After all, like a separate and impersonal reader, Saunders wanted to maintain his distance.

"And yes, I did just say 'ain't,'" Tom said.

Saunders looked directly at his face. His forehead had continued to sweat after removing the mask, but instead of wiping it, he just let the sweat drip off the tip of his nose. Was it an oversimplification to say Tom was crazy? That Tom could only express his angst with violence? Where was the line between Tom and Adam? Or Saunders and Tom? Or Tom and anyone for that matter? Hadn't Saunders also been seeking a violent solution, if only against himself? What was the line between Henry David Thoreau and Ted Kaczynski? Just a misfiring of synapses?

Both, after all, were teachers.

"I've always liked you, Berlin," Tom said. "You're a good guy. Hell, you even gave me your bag. Albeit, a little violently. But you're no different than them. I saw how you mocked me last time we met. I saw the pleasure in your eyes at the thought I'd be stuck hustling coffee the rest of my life."

If Saunders could say something, what would it be? I always liked you too, Tom. I've always thought you were a hardworking, good guy until you shot up my composition class this morning.

"But you knew it, Berlin. You knew it all along. Harry was never going to give me that job. So now it's my turn to do some mocking."

Saunders had already been evaluated once that day and didn't need another.

"You let yourself go, Berlin. You gave up. You took your eye off the ball. That's why Kathy left. No woman was going to respect that."

He noted Tom's use of a baseball cliché to critique him.

At least I was just going to kill myself, Saunders wanted to tell him. But you, you selfish bastard, decided to take innocent people with you.

"You lied," Tom said. "You always knew it, Berlin. Why did I believe you? I wanted it so badly I trusted you knew what you were talking about. But you lied. And you laughed about it. And I couldn't let you get away with it."

Tom stubbed out the cigarette on the classroom floor and Saunders watched as the cherry seeped in and singed the carpet. He noticed Tom's shoe smooshing the shit pellet left by the rabbit.

"I'm sorry," Tom said. "I'm sorry for what I've done to you."

Saunders felt compelled to get up and show Tom that he hadn't done a goddamn thing to him. That he'd failed at his task to even shoot him. But when he tried to move his body, he felt enormously weak and fell right back to the ground.

"I don't deserve to live," Tom said.

Saunders opened his mouth to say something.

"Water," he whispered.

"Berlin," Tom said, standing up. "Berlin! Hang on. Don't go anywhere yet."

Maybe it'd be better if Tom just shot him than to have to depend on him like this. Saunders heard Tom rummaging through the backpacks of students. And for the first time, he dared to look around.

The classroom was empty.

"They fled, Saunders," Tom told him, coming back with a water bottle he'd looted. "Just like they always do. It's the same thing every semester. They flee and they leave us here. For dead."

And Kathy? Had she also fled?

"The worst villains always do," Tom said. "Even Harry. But you know that. It's guys like you and I who have to stay and suffer all the consequences."

Then Tom was down on his knees, handing the water bottle to Saunders who managed to hold it up against his chest with his weak hand and tip it toward his lips.

"Look," Tom said, tilting his neck, "you're bleeding, Saunders. Goddamnit, you're bleeding."

He held the plastic bottle up to show Saunders the blood on it. Saunders looked down at his shirt. Blood had soaked through. Had the bullet not been intercepted by the book as he thought it had?

At least it wasn't Adam. That, he could be thankful for. Maybe it wasn't too late for Adam. Maybe he still had a chance. Maybe by dying this way, Saunders could be a hero from the grave.

"Do you think I'm a bad person, Berlin?" Tom said, grabbing one of the guns and pressing it against Saunders's temple. "Do you think I'm a bad teacher?"

When Saunders didn't answer, Tom got impatient.

"Well, do you?"

"No," Saunders could just barely whisper. His body was shaking. And he immediately regretted saying it. This could well be his very last statement. He was going to die a violent death at the hands of Tom Corona. Why had he lied?

Tom laughed.

"Liar, liar, pants on fire," he said, pressing the gun harder against Saunders's temple. Saunders remembered some research he had done. The temple was too risky and could leave him a drooling vegetable instead of killing him.

"It isn't right," Tom said. "To let a man die slowly."

He cocked the gun. Adam had once told Saunders this was mostly done for effect in Hollywood movies. Still, what a perfect verb for it, *cocked.*

"Truth be told, Saunders," Tom said. "You already died a long time ago."

He squeezed the trigger. Click. Nothing. Tom laughed.

"Fuck me," he said, tossing the gun across the room. "The chamber's empty. How does it feel to be lied to, Professor?"

Just then, they heard noises on the roof that sounded like footsteps. Tom stood up.

"They're coming," he said, quickly grabbing the other gun off the floor and barricading himself behind the classroom door.

"It's the end of the line now, Berlin. What kind of name is that anyway? *Ber-lin*?"

He aimed the gun at Saunders.

"Pew! Pew! Pew!" he said, then started laughing again. "*Berrrr-lin.*"

Tom shook his head.

"Hey," he said. "How about this one? Wanna see something funny?"

When Saunders didn't respond, Tom called him again.

"Hey, *Ber-lin*," he said, looking towards the door as if expecting that at any minute someone would be coming. "Hey. I'm asking you a question. Wanna see something funny?"

Saunders thought he heard voices outside the classroom. Would they be too late?

"Hey," Tom said, glancing back at the door, before turning to face Saunders. "Hey, *Professor*. I said, wanna see something funny?"

Before Saunders could turn away, Tom stuck the gun in his own mouth and squeezed the trigger. This time, the chamber wasn't empty. The bullet ripped through Tom's sweaty face, splattering blood and bone and brains all over the wall decorated with the Chinese proverb.

Death wasn't glorious. Death was messy. Impersonal. Not a peaceful escape from the world, but a bunch of bodily fluid. Death was a lie.

"I'm sorry," Saunders said aloud, as if apologizing to his students.

He threw up.

Then he reached for the water bottle left on the floor in front of him. As he washed the taste of puke out of his mouth, Saunders saw the rabbit, shivering in the corner, its white fur sprayed red, its ears flattened. Goddamn rabbits. Then he heard more footsteps on the roof. Help was coming. He felt the wound in his chest, then looked at his hand. More blood. On the floor lay his copy of *Au Revoir*, red fingerprints smeared across Harry and Kathy's author photos.

Today was only Monday.

He thought of that old eighties song by the Boomtown Rats: *I don't like Mondays/ I don't like Mondays/ I don't like Mondays/I want to shoot-oo-oo-oot, the whole day down.*

At some point, he must have lost consciousness, because he awoke to what sounded like an army amassing somewhere outside the classroom. He felt weak, but his body had stopped shaking as if someone had wrapped him in a soft warm blanket. Even his eye wasn't twitching.

Did he regret coming to class this morning? In some ways, of course. Not in the least for the sake of his students who were no doubt traumatized. As for him, it was different and not because he had been looking for a way to kill himself. He didn't regret coming to class this morning for another reason altogether, something he had always longed for as a citizen of this great nation. Lying on the floor of this classroom, for the first time ever, Berlin Saunders felt like a true participant in American life.

He closed his eyes again.

Soon the SWAT team would enter, followed by the paramedics who would lift him up onto a stretcher and rush him to the hospital. Soon he would be wheeled into the emergency room where surgeons would be waiting. The doctors, the nurses, the paramedics – they knew what they were doing. After all, they had been trained for this.

He could hear them coming. Ambulances were now crossing the parking lot. Helicopter propellers turning somewhere above his head. Maybe once grades were submitted, he'd take a trip this summer. Put it all on a credit card. Maybe go to England. Or Mexico. Or France. Or the Balkans. Maybe someplace exotic, a tropical island where he could sit on a beach and sip frozen cocktails. Decompress a bit. Things had been hard this spring. Much too hard. But they would only get better. Soon the mayor would arrive and stand at a podium and speak through a microphone. The president would address the nation. The whole world would want to know his story. It wouldn't be much longer now. The semester was finally over. All he had to do was wait. And trust in the professionals.

<h1>Acknowledgements</h1>

Grateful acknowledgment is made to the following people: Diliana Stamatova for her love, support, and patience; Gary Anderson and everyone at Run Amok for their belief in this novel; my colleague-in-arms Robert Guffey, for his mad copy editing skills; Rebeca Ladrón de Guevara and Larry Raymond Duncan, for their suggestions and encouragement after reading some of the earliest drafts (also for taking me to see the liberty bell); Wyn Cooper, for helping me trim the fat and stick to the story; my mentors Rafael Zepeda, Stephen Cooper, and John Rechy; all my friends, family members, and editors who have supported me over the years; and lastly, to my student veterans, some of the bravest and brightest I have ever had.

Clint Margrave is the author of two poetry collections, *Salute the Wreckage* (2016) and *The Early Death of Men* (2012), both published by NYQ Books. He lives in Los Angeles, CA.